Claude Monet Designs Yankee Stadium
A Love Story

R. Lee Procter

Black Rose Writing | Texas

ISBN: 978-1-68513-205-7
PUBLISHED BY BLACK ROSE WRITING
www.blackrosewriting.com

Printed in the United States of America
Suggested Retail Price (SRP) $19.95

Claude Monet Designs Yankee Stadium - A Love Story is printed in Garamond Pro

*As a planet-friendly publisher, Black Rose Writing does its best to eliminate unnecessary waste to reduce paper usage and energy costs, while never compromising the reading experience. As a result, the final word count vs. page count may not meet common expectations.

I dedicate this book to my hero, Claude Monet.
Emphysema, glaucoma, cataracts—he still got up every morning
to show us what an astonishing world this is.

Grateful thanks to Matt Solari, Steven Smith,
Gil Reavill and Haris Orkin

Faux-Monet cover art by the great Joe Dea

Claude Monet Designs Yankee Stadium
A Love Story

*"Against the ruin of the world,
there is only one defense:
the creative act. "*
–Kenneth Rexroth

CHAPTER ONE

October 3

Melvin Flack was invisible. Well, no; he was definitely *there*: a fifty-eight-year-old silver-thatched Security Guard in a lumpy blue blazer. And yet, every day, thousands of visitors to the Metropolitan Museum of Art looked past him, around him, and through him. Why would anyone look at him when "Starry Night" by Vincent Van Gogh was around here someplace? He'd outlived his rage about this, leaving a residue of dread. Weeks went by without a single adult acknowledging him. Who'd notice if he actually disappeared?

He was surprised to discover the grace inside this curse. His duties were to show up and...what exactly? When he was hired, his supervisor, Dwayne Mallard told him, "Just keep the peckerwoods from flicking their boogers at the Van Goghs." If he caught a visitor trying to gouge a fingernail of souvenir pigment off a Degas, he was empowered to "take all necessary steps" to stop that guest, short of doing something that would foment viral outrage on social media. Since every guest now had a video camera in her smartphone, Mel took this to mean "inform management and back away."

So now he was paid to stroll through the Annenberg Galleries and loiter in Room 821. Here he could stare at the paintings of his hero/tormentor, Claude Monet. Hero because Monet had triumphed at the task that had defeated Mel. Tormentor because Mel had never buried the corpse of his ambition. He had come here – right here, on this same walnut bench he was sitting on now – when he was eight, and, in a blink, he saw his destiny. *Wow! I want to do that. Exactly that. Paint pictures like that. Make the whole world come alive.* And for the next fifty years life conspired in a thousand tiny ways and few colossal ones to obliterate his simple dream.

"'Scuse me, but…are you okay?" Uh-oh. Mel blinked, checked his face. Hot tears running down both cheeks. *Who's asking? A boy. About seven. I can handle this.*

"Ummm, no, it's just…allergies. Happens every fall." He dabbed his face with a handkerchief and looked at the boy. Blue ninja uniform with the jacket cowl pushed back, showing sandy blonde hair. Mel noticed a woman – the boy's mother, he guessed – twenty feet away grazing on the other mid-career Monets: the Rouen Cathedral, the poplars, Morning on the Seine, the Japanese Bridge at Giverny. A four-year-old girl in a banana-gold princess gown, light-up sneakers, and a sparkly tiara was looking up at her hot pink "Happy Birthday Princess!" balloon.

"I don't get this picture," said the boy. He was staring at the haystacks.

"What's not to get?" said Mel.

"What's the big deal about it? Why is it here?"

Kids, thought Mel. *They go right for it.* "Great question. And I've got the answer."

The kid turned to Mel, surprised. "You do?"

Mel nodded. "I was hangin' with the painter who did this."

"Really?"

Mel did the math. If he was twenty in 1891, that'd make him a hundred and forty-five. "Really," he said. "Know anything about this guy Claude Monet?" The boy shook his head. *Whew.* "Here's what he told me." He leaned close to the boy, ready to reveal the secret. "Look at it."

"Okay." The boy turned his head and stared at the painting.

"He said to me, 'Mel?' That's my name by the way. What's yours?"

"Logan." He continued to stare at the picture.

"'Mel,' said Monet, 'any hack can paint a cathedral, or a rose garden or a sunset and make it look beautiful. But a haystack? Who looks twice at a haystack? I'm going to paint the most boring thing I can find and capture it right at sunset, like it's on fire with red and gold light and then maybe everybody will wake up!"

"Wake up?" The boy's blue eyes were wide.

"Look at it, Logan. Look at the way he captured the light. Really look. Monet is saying, 'The world is full of beauty, it's everywhere! Even a haystack! *Especially* a haystack!'"

"Uh huh." Logan wasn't convinced, but he was still staring at it.

"You like art? Like to draw?"

"Yeah. A little. I'm, uhhh, not very good." He grimaced, and Mel frowned. Kids were creative geniuses, and Mel could tell the school system was already de-geniusing Logan.

"Me too. Or at least I did. Now I just, you know, *look* at them. Especially this one. It's so full of…" Mel's walkie-talkie squawked to life. "'Scuse me."

"Hey little buddy, we got a situation down here." Sam Dollar's gruff voice was taut, just short of panic. "Ground floor behind Medieval Hall. Level Five threat, code critical."

Holy shit. Mel keyed his mike. "On my way."

"It's the big one, Melvin. Nine-eleven Vee-Two. Bust it. Over."

Mel stood up and stuck his hand out. "That stuff about me hanging with Monet? Keep it between the two of us. Nice to meet you, and keep drawing, no matter what!" Then he took off at a dead run.

CHAPTER TWO

Mel sat in his boss's office, dazed, nursing two furious welts on his chest. Dwayne Mallard stared daggers at him as he yelled into his phone, "You're kidding me. You're KIDDING me!" Mel pressed a tissue over the alcohol pad on his wounds and waited for the Vicodin to kick in. His mind wandered back over the past twenty-four years. *What just happened? How did I end up here, chest on fire, lit up by my best friend?* He'd always wondered what it would be like to be tased. Now he knew. It was like Darth Vader stabbing you in the chest with his light saber. And the worst was yet to come. The Inquisition was about to begin.

"Okay. All right. So, what in blue blazes happened down there?" Dwayne Mallard was staring at Sam Dollar, Mel's beefy best friend. Dwayne was Interim Acting Associate Supervisor of Museum Operations. He was trying to assert his authority but the three qualifiers in his title undermined him from the get-go, and the threadbare comb-over and failed porn star moustache didn't help. He was no match for Sam, who lived by the Marine Corps tattoo on his bulging bicep: "Embrace the Suck." Sam was the one who had shot Mel with his Taser pistol.

"Look, ummm, this is all my fault," said Velocity Blake. She was a skinny twenty-something art geek in camo paints and Doc Martens.

"Okay then," said Mallard. "You first."

"Well, the MRs decided to…"

"Whoa, whoa, whoa," said Mallard. "The MRs? Who…"

"The Moist Robots. Our freegan art collective."

"Uh huh. Yes. Freegan. Okay." Mallard turned this over in his mind. "Go on."

"It was a prank. The Met is so, you know, pompous. We just wanted to play a little joke."

"*Joke?*" said Mallard.

"Yeah," said Velocity. "I mean, the Met is such a mausoleum. Art is supposed to be fun, right? Wake people up, not put 'em to sleep. So, we decided to put on our *own* exhibition at the Met. Our latest stuff, for a flash mob of our pals. For a half an hour. In the women's bathroom on the ground floor, across from the cafeteria. Guerilla art. In, out, nobody the wiser…"

"And how were you going to accomplish this, if you don't mind me…?"

Sam Dollar cut him off. "I can answer that. At fourteen-thirty hours, yours truly saw a pack of shifty-eyed young males enter the Museum. To a man they fit the profile for suicide bombers per the Department's post-9/11 security training." *This is Sam's sweet spot*, thought Mel. *He knows this shit backwards, forwards, upside down, and sideways.*

"Suicide bombers?" said Velocity, eyes wide with surprise. Sam smirked. Mallard turned pale.

"Let's go down the list that you personally issued my department, shall we, Sir?" said Sam. "Age of these alleged perps? Eighteen to thirty. Checklist of suspicious qualities? Multiple layers of clothing, including soiled overcoats inappropriate to late summer? Check. Robotic walk? Eyes downcast? Lack of mobility in upper torso as if constricted by possible explosive device? Check, check, check. Failure to respond to authoritative commands, instead walking with deliberation toward objective? Big ol' honkin' checkety-check check."

"Except," said Mallard, "they were smuggling paintings, not bombs."

"And I'm supposed to know that *how*, Sir?"

Dwayne turned to Mel. "And where were you while Mister Dollar was routing these Jihadis?"

"I was, oh, you know…"

"Annenberg Galleries, am I right? Woolgathering on duty? Parked on a bench, mooning over your precious Monets?"

Busted. Mel leaned forward, sending another dagger of pain into his chest. He gulped, then rallied. "I was on duty, serving the public when Officer Dollar buzzed me about a possible situation on the ground floor past the Medieval Gallery. As I arrived, I saw Ms. Blake walk into the women's restroom and push a custodial cart into the doorway. Then I saw these scruffy kids in big overcoats running toward that restroom, with Sam right behind them."

"What did you think they were up to?" said Mallard.

Mel wanted to spin this into something credible without getting Sam fired. "Sam is our go-to guy on this stuff…"

"Did they look to you like suicide bombers?"

"Well…"

"Of course not! These were…I don't know…HIPPIES, for gawd's sake!"

"Hippies?" said Mel. He frowned. He'd grown up with hippies. "These weren't hippies."

"I think you mean 'slackers,'" said Velocity.

"Okay, whatever," said Mallard.

"And we are *not* slackers," insisted Velocity. "The Moist Robots are focused, industrious citizens, participating with vigor in the civic life of our city."

"You're troublemakers," huffed Mallard.

"Sir? Can I just finish my report?" said Sam.

Mallard sighed, rolled his eyes at the ceiling. "Go ahead."

"As per our training," said Sam, "I assessed the threat as level five, code critical. I tracked the suspects, observed them infiltrating the aforementioned women's comfort station. I ordered them to cease their activities, come out and put their hands behind their heads, fingers laced. They failed to comply and became verbally abusive. I entered the bathroom followed closely by Officer Flack and observed our female suspect here, Ms. Velocity Blake, pushing what I ascertained to be C-4 explosive into the walls."

"Only it *wasn't* C-4, *was it*, Mister Dollar?"

"Congratulations, Sir."

"For what?"

"For the impeccable twenty-twenty hindsight of a pencil-pushing desk jockey." Mallard levitated out of his chair and pointed at Sam, ready to drop the guillotine blade. Velocity cut him off.

"It was poster putty. So our pictures would stick to the walls."

"But it looked just like…anyone could see…I mean, the optics were undeniable," said Mel.

Mallard sat down and turned to him, bewildered. "You're defending this man? After he assaulted you with his Taser weapon?"

"From what I could see, the very existence of this institution was at risk!" shouted Sam.

Mallard exploded. "And that's why you, Officer Dollar, drew down on a guest, Ms. Blake here, with that…that…"

"Stun-Der-Matic XL 77, sir. The electroshock side arm of choice for elite law enforcement."

"A weapon explicitly prohibited for use inside the walls of this institution! A fact of which you are very well aware!"

"Oh yeah, fine," sneered Dollar. "Museum policy. Neutralize bomb-wielding malefactors with a frowny face and a devastating put-down. You don't want to see what goes into the meatloaf? Stay out of the mess tent, SIR!"

Mel thought Sam might rush Mallard and break him like a breadstick. "Look!" he shouted. Everyone turned to him. "Sam was just doing what this place trained him to do…with the possible exception of the stun gun."

"Okay," said Mallard, desperate to get this thing back on track. "So now Sam is in the bathroom, aiming that, that *thing* at Ms. Blake." He turned to Sam, who was snorting like a Pamplona bull. "What caused you to…to…"

"I ordered Ms. Blake to cease her activities and lie prone on the floor in accordance with institutional policy."

Mallard turned to Velocity. "And what did you do?"

"I, ummm…well, I guess I laughed."

"Laughed?" said Mallard, stupefied.

"Yeah. I mean, Captain America comes at me with his whoopee-do zap gun? For putting some pictures up in a lady's john? The whole thing was just so, you know, silly."

Mallard gazed at her. "Silly. Right." Then he turned to Mel. "And that's why you stepped in front of Ms. Blake? Because you knew this would set off Officer Dollar?"

"Yeah. I didn't want her to get, you know…"

"He's my hero," said Velocity. "He saved my butt. And my chest. Maybe my life."

"I lost my shit, Sir," said Sam. "Entirely my bad. You want to sack me for a series of flawed but entirely justified judgment calls, have at it."

"That's exactly what I'm…"

"NO!" shouted Mel. "A guy makes one mistake…"

"One mistake?" yelled Mallard. "ONE? Do you know how many parents I've had to mollify because your colleague manhandled their children?"

Sam erupted. "Their children, yeah, those innocent little crumb crushers who are stealing us *blind*, Sir! The gift shop is a war zone. We're losing 53 King Tut pencil cases a day, 31 of those Egyptian porcelain hippos, and forget about the Edvard Munch key fobs! You want to stop that shit, you need a viable deterrent. That'd be Sam Dollar."

"Not any longer, Mr. Dollar," said Mallard. He straightened himself up for The Speech. "The Metropolitan Museum has a mission to collect, preserve, study, exhibit, and stimulate appreciation by our guests for works of art that glorify the highest achievement of mankind. Our mission is NOT, as you seem to believe, to harass our guests, and terrorize them with contraband electroshock weapons. Therefore, I am going to recommend that you be separated from this institution, and that your friend Mr. Flack be suspended indefinitely until…"

"Ahem…" All eyes swiveled toward the stentorian throat clearance in the doorway. Dwayne Mallard continued to move his mouth for three seconds, but nothing came out. Then, finally, a hoarse whisper.

"Mr. DeWolfe! Wow! I didn't...I haven't...please come in, sir. Please."

Van Courtland DeWolfe was a Vanity Fair photog's dream of a patrician New York one-tenth-of-one-percenter: tall and slender, full head of lustrous silver hair, impeccably accoutered in a grey bespoke three-button suit. He was everything Dwayne Mallard dreamed of becoming but never, ever would.

"Hi, Grampa," said Velocity. *Grampa?!?* Mel looked at Mallard, a nuclear reactor in Chernobyl mode.

"G-grampa?" Mallard rasped.

"Hello, Vee." DeWolfe turned to Mallard. "I understand there was a bit of a kerfuffle on the ground floor."

"Kerfuffle. Yes. Oh, yes sir," said Mallard, babbling. "I'm here, umm, un-kerfufflizing, Mr. DeWolfe, sir."

"Really? How?" DeWolfe looked dourly at Mallard. A single arched eyebrow said, *And when you answer, remember that I'm a Museum Trustee and major contributor to the endowment. And that I'm on a first name basis with Chase Hancock, the Director of the Metropolitan Museum. And with a single phone call I can send you back where you came from, supervising the lunch shift at the Applebee's in the Staten Island Mall.*

Mallard swallowed hard. "This Security Officer used an unauthorized weapon that caused..."

"Velocity," said DeWolfe, ignoring Mallard.

"Yes, Grampa?"

"This is one of your capers gone awry, is it not?"

She bowed her head and nodded. "Yes, sir."

"Is this really the best use of your time?"

"No, sir."

DeWolfe turned to Mallard. "Any property damaged?"

"Uhhh, no, I don't..."

"Guests injured?"

"No guests. But Officer Flack..." Mallard motioned toward Mel.

"I'm fine, Sir," croaked Mel.

DeWolfe nodded. "Chase and I had a chinwag. Guests are already tweeting pictures from this debacle, and five television news crews are downstairs sniffing for dirt. You, Mister Mallard, are going to stand before the assembled media, smile, and spin this as a light-hearted prank. The Metropolitan Museum is *pleased* about young people taking such an *interest* in what we do. Oh, we have such a jolly good sense of humor about ourselves!"

"What about…" He pointed at Sam Dollar.

"Any disciplinary action will betray our narrative and show up online. I'm certain Officer Dollar is chastened and will readily agree to relinquish his unsanctioned sidearm."

Sam looked deeply into DeWolfe's eyes, and Wolfey looked back. The message was clear. *I'm as serious as a heart attack, and it won't be my heart attack.* Sam said, "I will indeed, Sir. With my apologies."

"Contrition! Excellent." DeWolfe turned back to Mallard. "I'm handing this back to you. Leave my granddaughter and the rest of the…errr…"

"Moist Robots."

"Yes. Leave them out of it. No names, just some young art lovers who got carried away. We've gifted them with free passes to enjoy the Museum in a more conventional manner."

"Yes, sir."

DeWolfe stared at Mel. "Do you require emergency care?"

"No, sir."

"Take appropriate measures to resolve your trauma and proffer the bill to Dwayne here. The Museum will pay. Might I at least get you a cab back to your living quarters?"

"No," said Mel. "I'll walk. Autumn in New York and all that."

"I'll walk him home, Grampa," said Velocity.

"Splendid," said DeWolfe. He focused on his granddaughter. "Why do I put up with you?"

"Ummm…because I remind you of you?"

DeWolfe laughed. "Oh. Yes, of course. And I'm assuming we're still on for lunch tomorrow?"

"Sure."

"I suppose lunching here in the Trustee's dining room…"

"It's my turn to choose, remember?" said Velocity. "I found the most amazing food truck: Korean fusion barbecue. They make bulgogi-kimchi soft tacos that'll change your life."

DeWolfe sighed heavily. "I don't wish my life to change. That said, I'll see you then."

CHAPTER THREE

Thanks to the miracle of prescription pain medication, Melvin Flack was loving his walk home with Velocity. Sam Dollar – warrior, ally, healer – had fixed him up with a 30 mg dose of morphine from his personal military-issue stash, and Mel was skiing behind the rocket-powered dreamboat of that delightful dose. Morphine! All Hail Morpheus, Greek god of dreams! Mel was waltzing homeward, bathed in the yellow-gold haze of an October dusk.

"Mel? Did you hear what I said?" asked Velocity.

"No, sorry. I was just...just remembering that first moment when I fell in love with New York. God, how I miss it."

"But...you're here, now," said Velocity. "You actually live here."

"I DO? Then I gotta get out of here! How can I miss New York if I won't leave?"

A laugh. "You're weird."

Mel skipped in front of her, waving his arms. "Me? Weird? Coo-coo bananas freegan art collective girl who just happens to be the freaking granddaughter of Gotham City's biggest cultural big shot? What the hell is a freegan, anyway?"

"We live for free. We live off what other people throw away. In dumpsters and stuff."

"No shit?"

"No shit. We pretend it's a, you know, political statement. Truth is, we're just troublemakers who get off on dumpster diving. Plus, we love the freedom. Free to make the art we want, all day long, off the grid. That's why I'm the only relative Grampa talks to. I couldn't care less about his millions."

"Uh huh. So, what did you say earlier? That thing I missed?"

"I just asked if you'd always been a security guard, or if you'd been, I don't know...."

Mel smiled. He was sick of telling this story, so he let the morphine speak for him while he wafted along. "Velocity – a name I love, by the way – there are two paths to enlightenment. Do you know what they are?"

"No. Illuminate me."

"Well, first there's the High Road. That's for religious mystics, cultural visionaries, elementary school teachers, and artists in our beloved Metropolitan Museum of Art. I sense that you are on the High Road, opting out of the American nightmare of mindless consumerism in pursuit of a more principled way of being in the world."

"That's kind of grandiose, but, yeah, okay. And the low road?"

"That's my path. Where the seeker finds his spiritual destiny by stumbling into every manhole that fate puts in front him."

"Uh huh. Like what?"

"Like I let my mother kill my ambition to become a painter. I let my father dictate my major in college: business administration. Oh, man. I might as well have majored in theoretical physics. I minored in fine art, but even that was a manhole."

"How so?"

"To me, the Impressionists are...well, I love them. I always wanted to be one. Get inside their technique, learn their secrets, and do what they did. Nope. To pass, I had to pretend to like what my professors liked, which was Abstract Expressionism. By the time I graduated I didn't know who I was or what I liked, so I dove headfirst into the biggest manhole of all: romantic love. I'll find my soul mate! True happiness! Together forever!"

"I'm guessing that didn't work out..."

Mel looked at the late afternoon sky. *What's that shade? I'd call it flaming pumpkin...* "Forever lasted about three years, followed by ten years of boredom and two years of nuclear war. What a train wreck."

"You're pretty hard on yourself."

Mel stopped. Velocity turned back to him. He looked at her, suddenly sobered. "No. You're wrong. I remember that twenty-three-year-old kid and have nothing but compassion for him. He was doing the best he could. He just didn't know what he didn't know." He breathed in, pulling himself back into the present. He filled his lungs with the sweet scent of New York street pizza. Eyes right: Germano's thin crust, a fresh pie in the steamed-up window. "Want a slice?"

"I'm good." They started walking again. "Then what happened?"

"Ahhh," said Mel. "The next manhole. Advertising! I got a job in the ad biz where I perverted what talent I had to sell gossip magazines, horsemeat hamburgers, and fruit-flavored beer."

"Yeow!" Velocity blanched. "Is there such a thing?"

"Was, for about four months. This was the golden age of wine coolers, so our client said, 'Why not raspberry beer?'"

"Because it's, ummm...disgusting?"

Mel laughed. "Best way to kill a bad product? Do great advertising for it. People tried it, hated it, and our client poured three hundred million dollars of fruit-infused malt liquor down the Milwaukee sewer system. And my advertising career went down the sewer with it, along with my marriage. Was I despondent? NO! I was free!"

"Free?"

"Free to become the starving artist I'd dreamed of becoming. I sub-let 278 square feet of a rent-controlled apartment and cranked out twenty-two paintings in sixteen months."

"Wow!"

The sky had darkened to a rich shade of dark raspberry. "Most fun I ever had. Lived on coffee, tuna sandwiches, ramen, and jug wine. I'd get up at dawn, throw paint on canvas all day, then walk down Bleecker Street splattered with pigment, the ghost of Jackson Pollock. I was finally ready for my storm-the-art-world coming-out show. 'The Art of M. Durward

Flack – Impressions of New York' at Dave's Palette Shop, Greenwich Village, New York, June 17, 1994. I'm sure you remember it." He looked at her and got the blank stare he expected.

"Sorry."

"Come now, you must. Let me repeat the date. June 17, 1994." Another blank look, with a headshake. "O.J.? White Bronco? America glued to the television? Art show attendance craters to near zero?" Her eyes went wide. She understood.

"Oh. Oh my."

Mel laughed. "Seven people showed up. Five were from the bar next door, looking for a bathroom. That's when I gave up."

"Why?"

"Why what?"

"Why'd you give up? That was a tough break, but I mean…well, it sounds like you were having fun. Don't you like painting?"

"I love painting. I hate failing."

Damn! Mel could feel the morphine high start to abate. The Black Cherry sunset blinked off into nighttime. "Every time I drag out my stuff and go to Central Park and find the perfect spot and lift my hand to the canvas, all I can think about is how much I've lost. How good I could have been. How nobody likes my work and how much better every painting is that I look at every day at the Met. I can't hear myself think over my brain screaming at me. I've given up. It's over. I no longer fight being a failure. I *embrace* my loser-dom. C'mon, I'm the kind of guy who gets tased by his best friend."

This was the Master Narrative of his life, the digital audio file that played in an endless loop in his brain. He was the hero of the story: he'd stopped trying to be anything more than the doormat upon which The Binding Force of the Universe wipes its feet.

Still, hearing himself tell the story had an unsettling effect. He just sounded pathetic. He wondered what part of the presentation he should re-think. Was it the story itself, or how he told it?

CHAPTER FOUR

"What was that address again?" asked Velocity, baffled. Mel raised his eyes expecting to see his building. What he saw was chaos. A spasm of bile bubbled up in his throat. The faint euphoria he'd been savoring flipped into a sick shiver of nausea.

Suddenly this day had two parts. The tasing was just Part One: Prelude to Homelessness. Now, the climax.

A lavender "Cartage by Cheesebrook" private-haul garbage truck loomed just ahead. A pair of squat garbage men in stained magenta overalls came out the door of his apartment. The stubby one was toting two five-foot roles of canvas – Mel's life's work – one on each shoulder. The dumpy one was hoisting Mel's mahogany studio easel with one hand, with his palette, paint kit and sketch pads in the other. They walked around a "Live @ Five" news truck to an orange dumpster. Stubby flipped the textile cylinders into the battered steel receptacle. Dumpy then ditched the easel and paint gear. Stubby waved at the driver, who activated the hydraulic mantis-arms to lift the metal bin up and over the cab and deposit Mel's meager life's work in the truck's mammoth hopper.

A jagged "NOOOOOOOOOOO!" welled up from the core of his being as Mel ran toward the cataclysm. A perplexed Velocity followed close behind.

Mel bumped the young female television newsie interviewing his landlord. He leapt onto the running board of the truck as the driver yanked the lever to pulverize the trash in the hopper. "Stop! That's my…" The bored driver's leather-gloved hand muffled Mel's last word. Mel could feel Lord Vader's light saber impale his chest a second time as he crashed backwards onto the pavement. His vision blurred as he watched the truck joggle. The packer blade inside the hopper crushed his life's work, melding it with a half-ton of pizza rinds, soiled diapers, and cigar butts.

Mel gasped for breath. He felt woozy from the red-hot welts that seared his chest. He looked up and saw his Judas landlord, Frank Pomeroy, bantering with a blonde reporter in a black mini skirt.

A fresh wave of outrage adrenalized Mel. He vaulted up and crashed the live shot, poking Pomeroy in the zipper of his powder-blue jumpsuit. "You sold me out, you bastard! Twelve years and now this! Why didn't you call me at work? They're throwing out my shit and you're not stopping them!"

"Wha…wait! Calm down!" blurted Pomeroy.

The reporter seized this as a career-making viral YouTube opportunity. "Ladies and gentlemen, a fight has just broken out, LIVE where billionaire developer Holcombe Parkes has just paid Greenwich Village resident Frank Pomeroy fourteen million dollars to vacate his rent-controlled apartment …"

"Fourteen MILLION?" screamed Mel, incredulous.

"He's crazy! Stop him! POLICE!" screamed Pomeroy, windmilling his arms for balance.

"Sir, if I can ask you a question, who are you and why are you assaulting Mister Pomeroy?"

"Because this idiot…he's my landlord. He had no right…"

"He's lying! I've never seen this guy…" barked Pomeroy into the camera.

"He's gouging me eight hundred bucks a month to sub-let the dank, miserable, cockroach-infested hallway of his putrid little apartment," said Mel.

"He's crazy! I would never…that's illegal! He's a psycho! He's got a gun! Stop him!" screeched Pomeroy.

Out of the corner of his eye, Mel could see uniforms hustling toward him. "My paintings! He let them throw them away like they were garbage! That's my life's work!"

At that moment the worst toupee in the history of male vanity stepped in front of Mel. The reporter was thrilled. "Here's the man who paid all that money for this place, controversial developer Holcombe Parkes."

Parkes looked directly into the camera lens and grinned. "Another monster win for Team Parkes, and for New York. Took me seven years to get this place, and now it's MINE. We're gonna tear down this dump, create 212 incredible new units."

"Condominiums?" said the reporter.

Parkes smirked. "I call 'em condo-MAXIUMS." He nudged the reporter, chortling at his own joke. "Places for this city's high-achieving elite mover-shakers, like me. I'm going to call it 'Parkes Place.' It's going to generate jobs, revenue, and pride that will benefit all my fellow New Yorkers." Parkes jerked his thumb backwards at Mel. "And say goodbye to the psycho street trash."

Psycho street trash? Mel wanted to head-butt this smug weasel, but Parkes's cadre of rent-a-cops grabbed him. He struggled, then a spike of chest pain defeated him. All he could do was stand there and watch Parkes finish his televised victory lap. The blonde buttoned her report with, "Holcombe Parkes, swashbuckling real estate kingpin, proving just how far he'll go to get what he wants, spending millions to make millions!"

Parkes? *Swashbuckling kingpin?* Parkes was a spotlight-hogging egomaniac with the gravitas of a Macy's parade balloon. His minions dropped Mel and marched off with their boss. Velocity knelt, opened his shirt and used a fistful of wet Starbucks napkins to soothe the wounds above his heart.

Mel was numb. He'd fallen down another manhole on the low road, sucker-punched by a smug douchebag. What was next? Locusts?

"Can you stand up?" Yes, he could stand up...or could he? It took Velocity a good twenty seconds to get Mel on his feet. "C'mon, I'll take you home with me."

"Okay, but...ummm...something I gotta do first," he said, heading for the remains of his ex-micro-dwelling. Velocity followed.

CHAPTER FIVE

Gone. Everything gone. His paltry life had been ransacked. The futon, the hot plate, the beat-up cruiser bike, the ancient Dell computer, the IKEA side table – gone.

"Oh, Mel..." He turned. Velocity was standing over a battered mop-wringer bucket, fishing a wadded-up canvas out of two inches of gray water. She handed it to Mel who unfurled it. He stared at it for twenty seconds, then knelt and spread it on the dingy avocado shag carpet. Then he wept.

The canvas Velocity had handed Mel was rolled-up and lodged in the crook of his arm as he trudged to the subway station with Velocity. She'd graciously offered to put Newly Homeless Man up at the Love Shack, a derelict Bronx apartment building that was the current home of the Moist Robots Art Collective. She wanted the story of the painting, so...

"I told you about my art show," said Mel. "I was almost ready, but I needed one more killer canvas for the front page of the New York Times Sunday Art Section. I asked myself, 'What would Monet do?'"

"What *would* Monet do?" asked Velocity.

Mel smiled. "Monet would pack up his kit, park himself in the middle of nature's chaotic wonder and throw what he saw on canvas. So that's what I did. I went to the Wedding Garden of the Queens Botanical Gardens. I sipped coffee and waited for...I didn't know what. Something.

Then..." He paused, dialing up the Technicolor hues of his memory-movie. "*She* walked into the garden. This young woman, I can see her now. Rosa."

"Rosa?"

Mel laughed. "That's what I called her, I have no idea what her real name was. Puerto Rican, probably sixteen. Young, fresh, round face, a little on the pudgy side. Her butterscotch-brown skin just, I don't know, *glowed*. She flounced around in a homemade white polyester wedding gown and a bridal hat covered with sequins and fake pearls, with a pouf of white tulle on the back. What I remember most, the thing that absolutely nailed me..." He stopped walking, back in that moment.

"What?" said Velocity.

He looked at her. "There's a sort of hope, a kind of cheerful, brainless optimism you can only have when you're sixteen and you still think all the sappy love songs and silly romantic movies are true. You don't understand that fate is waiting around the next corner with a tire iron, ready to work you over for the next, oh, fifty years." He willed himself back to that moment. "Her face...her smile...the easy way she laughed...I can see her now, so clearly. Just watching her glide around that garden chatting up her guests filled me with memories of what it was like to be young and happy and hopeful in a simple way. I couldn't stop staring at her and her bedraggled wedding party. The photographer? Dad with an Instamatic. I so wanted to hug her and say, 'Grab this with both hands, breathe it in, bank every moment in three dimensions, because you'll never, ever be as happy as you are right now. This is as good as it gets.'"

"But you didn't," said Velocity.

"No. But I did make it my business to get that moment on canvas. The eyes, so bright. The eyes and that radiant smile. Everything around me dropped away and I knew it was time to do what an artist does. I felt her joy. I seized it. I hurled it at the canvas with all the passion I could muster. I started with her eyes and smile and filled it in with oils. The whole wedding lasted about half an hour, and it ended with this lovely grace note. She'd kissed the groom, posed for pictures, drank the supermarket champagne, and now the wedding party was straggling out of the garden. For no reason I can fathom, the bride stopped, turned to me, and gave me this smart, carefree smile, like she knew what I was up to, like she and I were in cahoots. I smiled back and she nodded and turned away and caught up her friends and family and my heart fell out of my chest and broke into a million pieces. I knew I'd stay there for as long as it took to finish up because her lovely, round, hope-filled face was seared in my memory, and I was the only one who could capture that face in that garden on that day for all eternity."

"For what it's worth," said Velocity, "I think you did a good job. It's a great painting."

"I appreciate your kind words," said Mel, "and, with all due respect, I don't care what you think. I know it's the best thing I ever did. Maybe the only good thing."

"So…you never found out who that girl was?"

"Every once in a while, I think about tracking her down so I can give her the painting. Then I see myself knocking on the door of a slummy apartment and finding this meaty middle-aged woman with six crying kids and a husband in a wife-beater watching monster truck pulls and I wonder if that picture might just make her really, really sad. I think of looking into those beautiful brown eyes and seeing the grief and lost hope and broken dreams and I know that breaking her heart would break my own heart all over again."

CHAPTER SIX

On the walk to the subway station, Mel mused on his train wreck of a day. He felt like he'd been eaten by a pterodactyl and shat into the Popocatepetl Volcano, and now the chest pain was coming back. He'd spent his morphine tablet. Should he call Sam for another? Velocity said he'd find ample pain relief at the Love Shack.

He followed Velocity onto the A Train and communed with other doleful souls as the battered car clattered and swayed. He was thankful he was in the one place on earth where no one would be alarmed by – or even notice – a slightly seedy crime victim hunched over with pain, his ghost-white face a rictus of agony. What was it J.J. Hunsecker said at the beginning of "Sweet Smell of Success?" *"I love this dirty town."* Amen, brother.

The fourteen-block walk along the Grand Concourse to the Love Shack took them through a hundred years of architectural ambition and urban blight in the South Bronx. Velocity had researched the Shack, and her narrative of the building's rise, fall, and semi-rise kept Mel's mind off his travails.

Flo Ziegfeld wannabe Stanwyck W. Ziegler had built the nine-story Ziegler-Haversham Building in 1919 in lavish Beaux-arts style as housing for the legion of chorus girls he featured in "Ziegler's Zanies," a bi-annual series of Broadway "revue-sicals" that caffeinated Main Stem wickets during the Roaring 20s. Ziegler took the penthouse – the "Eagle's Nest," with a staircase winding upward to the rooftop "Whoopee Garden" – for himself and his headliner-mistress, Boopsie Baker. When the Zanies toured the hinterlands in odd-numbered years, Ziegler would rent the penthouse to Jazz Age notables, including Babe Ruth, Hizzoner Jimmy Walker, and Scott and Zelda.

The Great Depression bankrupted Ziegler and forced him to sell the building. For the next forty years the Z-H Building became a residence hotel for threadbare actors and playwrights dreaming of better days at the Algonquin. Then the building got swept up in the South Bronx horror show of the 1970s, devolving into a Section 8 welfare hotel that was abandoned completely in 1987.

The only reason that insurance grafting "fixers" didn't burn it down like the rest of the Bronx was Preston Ziff, fabled anarchist-beatnik-painter, avant-garde film critic and godfather of the freegan movement. Ziff claimed squatter's rights to the building. He recruited an army of frisky, freethinking fellow artists and formed his first "Zero" collective: zero drugs, zero rent, zero rules, and zero bullshit. The city of New York made a half-hearted attempt to evict these adventurous souls, but Ziff rallied public sentiment. Was the Mayor really going to throw out the plucky tenants of the only extant structure in a three-block radius, even as these residents were fighting off looters, fixing the place up, and offering free tours to like-minded cultural freebooters?

The Moist Robots took over in 2009, re-inventing the place for Millennials. The Robots used what funds they earned as artists to upgrade the eco-technology for the digital age. They also refined their "urban harvest" dumpster-diving practices to ensure a steady supply of food, water, and art supplies. "Our biggest fear," said Velocity as they walked up to the funky premises, "isn't failure. It's success. It's that we get Brooklynized."

"Brooklynized?" said Mel. "I don't..."

"You know. The artists move in 'cuz the rent is so cheap. Pretty soon the galleries will be here, and then the cafés and clothing boutiques, and pretty soon we're a thing. And then..."

"Starbucks," said Mel.

Velocity shivered. "An Apple Store, Pottery Barn, Baby Gap. Then a no-soul dirtbag like Holcombe Parkes buys up derelict buildings like ours and turns them into high-end condominiums which he sells for seven figures to investment bankers who want the artistic lifestyle without the mess or effort of creating, you know, art."

"Not condominiums," said Mel. "Condo-MAXIUMS."

She laughed. "Yeah. Then we have to find a new place and start over again."

Mel looked around. The Love Shack stood like a Jazz Age battleship in a jagged sea of potholed asphalt and trash-filled vacant lots, including a tumbledown ballpark moldering under a catawampus sign reading "Bojangles Field." "You really think…"

"We've heard rumors. We're already scouting property in Camden, New Jersey," said Velocity. She looked at her watch and grabbed Mel. "Hold it."

"What?"

"8:49, that's what. Perfect timing." Mel started to ask her what she was talking about, but her index finger touched her lips. "Just watch." Then she pointed to the building.

CHAPTER SEVEN

When Alice went through the Looking Glass, she met a queen who could believe six impossible things before breakfast. Mel's sixth thing that day was an atomic bomb blast that shattered the night air and demolished the ground floor of the building. Velocity caught Mel as he dropped his painting and staggered backwards. They both watched three more percussive bomb blasts shatter the fourth and fifth floors, imploding the building so each floor pancaked earthward. The "Eagle's Nest" penthouse kissed the earth with a final clap of thunder that echoed for a full twenty seconds, and Mel stared at a choking, gunmetal dust devil where a building had been a minute ago.

Velocity smiled at him. "Well? Cool?"

"C-cool?"

"You want to meet the guy who did that? He's my boyfriend. HEY DEMO!" A lanky dude – late twenties, 6'2", shaggy black mop top with a Van Dyke beard, black jeans, and a black hoodie – trotted toward them. He was hefting a homemade remote-control unit with a glowing green screen flanked by buttons, dials, sliders, and toggle switches. He handed the unit to Velocity and stuck out his hand.

"Demolition," he said. Mel shook it.

"You, ummm…wow. You did that?"

"Uh huh."

"Is that what you do for a living?"

"Pretty much. Like it?"

"Well…I, ummm…yeah, but…didja have to knock it down? I was kinda hoping…that is, Velocity told me I could sleep there tonight."

Velocity and Demo looked at each other and burst out laughing. Demo took back the unit, flicked up three toggle switches and punched the largest black button. The dust devil vanished along with the echo of the thunderclap. The Ziegler-Haversham Building aka the Love Shack was squatting right where it was supposed to be.

"Art, my friend. The modern miracle of 3D computer-generated projection mapping and ground-pounding 360 digital audio. My rig, my software, my work, entirely DIY."

"He lives to blow shit up," said Velocity. "It's what brought us together."

"When you're living in a world this ugly, ya gotta have a safety valve," said Demolition.

"He even gets paid for it," said Velocity, kissing her boyfriend on the cheek.

"Mostly party-hearty tech billionaires who want to blow up their summer homes to amuse their pals" smiled Demo.

Velocity handed Mel the painting he'd dropped, and the three of them walked toward the Love Shack.

• • •

"Excuse the noise," said Velocity as they walked through the Shack to the stairs. Mel had never seen such a hive of activity. Room after room featured a determined Millennial destroying the smug pretentions of establishment art. Painting (fine art, Pollock drip, and cubist), welding, and sculpting were just the beginning. Digital animators, performance artists, video directors and "laptronica" music producers were also hard at work. Each room had its own 110-decibel soundtrack with indie-rock battling techno, enhanced by the occasional blast of Metallica, U2, and Stax-Volt 60s Soul-Funk.

Demolition (formerly Dollar Bill Hitler, formerly Blunt Instrument, formerly Daytona Dave Dachau, originally Kevin Stevens of Wausau, Wisconsin) had his own studio where he designed his immersive digital cataclysms. After he showed that off, he bragged on what else he'd done for the Shack. His communal coffeehouse/library had over five thousand paperbacks rescued from library trash bins, bookstore dumpsters, and giveaway yard sales. The collection skewed heavily toward modern fantasy, classic Heinlein/Bradbury sci-fi, and "dying earth" dystopian fiction. Resident MRs reclined on curbside throw-out sofas and ratty wing chairs and rested their hot beverage mugs on a coffee table made of coffee table books pulverized in epoxy resin.

"Biggest challenge we have," said Demolition as they climbed toward the top floor, "well, two, really. First, we use a lot of juice for being off the grid. The MRs put solar panels on the roof and added a couple of wind turbines, but we still have to crank up the generators every so often. Got 'em running on veggie oil we get from Yo Mama, the local soul food joint next to Yankee Stadium."

"And then there's our poop and pee problem," said Velocity.

"Six composting toilets that make mulchy goodness for the veggie garden on the roof," bragged Demo.

Mel took it all in as he slogged upstairs. Artmaking on floors one, two, and three. Barracks-like six-to-a-room living quarters on four, five, six, and seven. The eighth floor was originally a ballroom, now a meeting room and kitchen. This is where the Robots figured out how to live and work without murdering each other. The kitchen featured tasty snacks like homemade kale chips, carrot sticks, hummus, and – very occasionally – some glorious atrocity rescued from a grammar school dumpster, like a Costco-sized bag of Double-Stuff Oreos.

Finally, the ninth floor "Eagle's Nest." The elevators hadn't worked since the Truman Administration and Mel made it his business to trudge up every step. Velocity had offered to let him sleep in her art studio on the first floor, but he refused. He wanted to be the Guy Even A Taser Couldn't Stop. Plus, *Scott and Zelda?* 'Nuff said.

Velocity began lighting votive candles with her Zippo, and Mel got his first real blink on the magnificent wreckage of Stanwyck Ziegler's love nest. He was surprised how much of the original penthouse décor survived. Moth-eaten crimson velvet curtains still veiled the arched windows. A stained satin Chesterfield and quartet of cracked red leather club chairs complemented those curtains. The white plaster walls were gouged, cracked, and crazed, with mossy-green stains like mammoth amoebas. The rotting remnants of the mahogany herringbone flooring revealed the concrete screed beneath. "From what I understand," said Velocity, "Ziggy left the day he went bankrupt in 1930. Didn't take a thing. New owners just sealed it off."

"Even Ziff didn't come in here," said Demo. "Took me half a day with a two-foot pry bar to get the damn door open. Spooky as shit when we walked in. This is pretty much the way we found it. Now we just use it as a place for friends of friends to crash."

Mel walked to one of the windows and pulled the curtains aside. The gloomy moonscape of the South Bronx was lit by a ring of glowing white lights in the near distance. "Yankee Stadium," said Velocity, just behind him.

"No," said Mel. "Not really."

"What?" said Velocity.

"There's only one Yankee Stadium for me, the first one. The House that Ruth Built," said Mel. "My Uncle Random used to take me to games there. This was the late 60s when the team was terrible, but we weren't there for the game. We were there to worship the Babe, the Mick, Yogi, Scooter, Whitey..." Mel felt Velocity and Demo staring at him. "A long time ago. Get a hot dog for fifty centers, a soda for a quarter. Now..."

"Fourteen bucks for a craft beer," said Demo. "What's up with that? I'd rather play ball than watch it. Soon as I get the Love Shack in shape, I'm gonna start in on that place across the street." Demo joined him at the window, and they both gazed down at the derelict ballpark Mel had seen coming in. It was a haunted house of torn fencing, broken windows and collapsed corrugated awnings.

"Bojangles Field," said Mel. "Bojangles. Is that, like..."

"Bill Robinson, the tap dancer, the one in that Shirley Temple movie. He built that place for his team, the Bronx Black Bombers. I found this book on Negro League baseball, has a whole thing about them. Joe Louis had a piece of the team too. They played from the early 30's to '46, had some decent years. Wait here, I found something over there you'll think is cool."

Demo vaulted out the door before Mel could stop him. Mel turned to Velocity. "Baseball fan?"

"I'm a roller derby chick. I'm sure you've heard of 'Bambi Skullcracker'? Jammer on the 'Eves of Destruction'?" Mel shook his head. "That's me. Demo is the president of my fan club."

Demo bounded back in with a hand-painted sign, silver letters on a pitted black tin. Mel read the words.

**On this spot in 1946,
Leroy "Satchel" Paige pitched a no-hit game
against Bob Feller's Major League All-Stars**

He looked at Demo. "Wow."

"Yeah," said Demo, looking down at the field. "Used to be a thing. Now you can barely make out the diamond 'cuz of all the gopher holes. It's nasty over there: skunks, raccoons, feral cats..."

"Demolition, my dear," said Velocity. "Enough. Let's get our guest ready for bed."

Mel now perched on the bedraggled couch as Demo and Velocity fixed him up for bedtime. Demo dragged in a well-used orange cousin to Mel's beloved Japanese Shiki-futon and billowed a flannel sheet on top of it. "Whaddaya think?"

"Luxury. I'm not worthy," said Mel. Then Velocity eased off his shirt, dabbed his welts with hydrogen peroxide and covered them with a gauze bandage. "You gonna be okay?"

"Never better," he said. "Except for...well, I know you don't have any morphine, but ummm..."

"We'll fix you right up," answered Demo.

Velocity produced a gray metal tackle box that folded out into six rusty trays of twelve bins, each one filled with pills, powders, and vials of syrup. "The MR pharmacy is now open. Doctor Demolition is this evening's consulting physician. Doctor? I believe a robust painkiller is indicated, complemented by a short-acting nonbenzodiazepine hypnotic of the imidazopyridine class."

"Let's not mess around," said Demo. "Five megs of Vicodin…"

"An Ambien," said Velocity.

"Half a Xanax…"

"All chased with a tumbler of Nyquil."

"Make it a double," said Demo. He smiled at Mel. "Don't worry. We kill pain, not people."

"Thanks," said Mel. *This'll knock me right out*, he thought. *Oblivion: bring it on.*

CHAPTER EIGHT

He couldn't sleep.

Damn.

After the narcotic cocktail he'd inhaled and all the shit he'd been through, he was *sure* he'd fall into a blissful coma thirty seconds after his head hit his balled-up chinos. Fat chance. His mind was racing. Once the gerbils started bouncing that plastic ball off the walls of his brain, he was a goner. The soul-deadening drum machine beat of industrial dance rivethead music throbbed through the floor.

Mel flung the sheet off the makeshift bed and sat up. This was his most feared mental state: too wired to sleep, too tired to think, and too flustered to doze. He'd be trashed in the morning, wandering the Met floor guzzling a jumbo coffee with five espresso shots to cover how wasted he was. Only he'd need more than coffee. He'd need a second Taser jolt.

Wait! There was something he could do: a task he could complete. The single votive candle still flickering on the floor revealed his hastily rolled up "Garden Bride, Queens" painting leaning against a serpentine twist of cast iron cradling a lead crystal ashtray. Mel had what he needed to christen the exclusive Melvin Durward Flack Exhibit Room at the Moist Robots Gallery of Contemporary Art.

Dozens of rusty, bent nails stuck out of the wall plaster. Mel chose the four least crooked ones and yanked them out by hand. He put the first nail in his mouth, ignoring the risk of tetanus. Then he grabbed the ashtray and unfurled his masterwork, holding it against the wall with his left elbow. He knew he should wait till dawn's first light, square it up properly and nail it as someone else held it for him. Better still, he should restore it to its original "show" condition: measured, stretched, and properly framed, then hung by wire from a single nail. *The hell with that.* Maybe getting this one thing done would generate the melatonin rush he needed to glide through the gates of slumberland.

He pushed the left side of the painting up with his elbow. He tried to eyeball it, to see if it met the "Fifty-Seven Inches on Center" eyeline guide for hanging art at the Met. *Oh, probably. What the hell. Who cares?* He pushed his face toward his left hand and took the nail out of his mouth with his thumb and index finger. His left arm was getting numb. *Gotta do this with one blow.* He positioned the nail in the left corner of the canvas, then grabbed the ashtray and bashed it.

CRUNCH. Crackle. Crash. Crumble.

Ooops.

Oh shit.

The blow punched a giant hole in the wall and crazed the plaster four feet in every direction. *Shit shit shit*, thought Mel. *This place survived ninety-one years in pristine shape, and inside ONE HOUR, I've managed to vandalize it.*

His face burned red. *How am I going to 'splain this to Demo, erstwhile building maintenance supervisor?* Very slowly, with bile burbling up in his gullet, he stuck his head in the hole to see if he could rescue some of the bigger chunks of plaster. He saw plenty of crumbly bits, some rotted lath beams...and something else. *What is that? A roll? Of...what? Carpet? Wallpaper? Or... Couldn't be.* He pulled his head out, blinked twice, then stuck it back in the hole. *A roll? Of canvas? Like his? What the hell? Probably the plans of this building, put here by the disgruntled architect after Ziegler stiffed him.*

Decision time. Mel could leave it till morning and get permission from V and D of Moist Robot High Command to open the wall, or he could cave in the crazed plaster, pull out whatever's in there and have a look. He surveyed the wall. He'd created a nasty-bad gash in the plaster already. He was wide-awake; buzzed, in fact, although he didn't know why. Morphine withdrawal? They'd have to fix the wall anyway, what difference did it make if the hole went from kinda biggish to mondo humongo?

Mel took the ashtray and pounded the ragged peak of the plaster hole. Another foot and a half crumbled away. A trio of crunching whacks opened a hole five feet deep and three feet wide. Mel surveyed his find. He was staring at a substantial roll of art canvas five feet high, with a nut-brown leather pouch perched on top. He plucked the leather bag off the paintings and ran his hands over it. *Wowsers.* Full-grain russet calf's skin with a bronze patina, still supple after how many years? He loosened the drawstring and pulled out a matching journal: calf's skin, fold-over design, bound with a leather wrap-tie. The wrap-tie snapped as he pulled on it, and the journal fell open to the title page:

Journal personnel de printemps 1921

He glanced at the bottom.

Claude Monet

He blinked and looked away. *MAN, that morphine is some powerful shit!* He looked back at the page. *Claude Monet.* What the hell? He'd suffered through three years of French in high school, but that was forty-five years ago. Let's see... *"Personal Journal of the Year 1921. Claude Monet."* He felt faint but he wasn't going to stop now. He turned the page.

" *Ce qui suit est mon compte d'un hasard extraordinaire qui a rempli les mois de mars à octobre 1921. Ce journal est un message dans une bouteille jetée sur les mers orageuses à lire, si jamais trouvé, comme une affirmation de ma probité artistique. Ma histoire est, en même temps, une histoire de mauvais calcul catastrophique et de la bonne fortune transcendante - de calamité et de bénédiction. Elle est,quand la nuit tombe, un asseveration que l'amour est un cygne noir, une circonstance absurde qui sauve les perdus et justifie la lutte infernale de l'artiste.* "

Amazing how things come back to you, like the music and lyrics from the "Patty Duke Show" theme, *"But Patty likes to rock and roll, a hot dog makes her lose control."* Best song lyric ever? He zeroed in on Monet's (or somebody's) scrawl, and the words reworked themselves from French to English in his mind.

"What follows is my account of a most extraordinary happenstance that filled the months of March to October, 1921. This journal is a message in a bottle cast upon stormy seas to be read, if ever found, as an affirmation of my artistic probity. My tale is, at the same time, a tale of catastrophic miscalculation and transcendent good fortune – of calamity and benediction. It is, as night falls, an asseveration that love is happiness: a black swan, an absurd circumstance that rescues the lost and justifies the hellish struggle of the artist."

The cranial POV camera of his personal mind-movie did a full Hitchcock Vertigo: pushed in and zoomed out at the same time. He felt vertigo, yes, but adrenalized vertigo, like what you'd feel in that split second of hang-time just after a homeless psycho pushed you off a subway platform and just before you splattered across the front of the BMT Canarsie Line.

BREATHE. He forced himself to take deep, slow, cleansing breaths. He was holding the diary like it was the single surviving dinner menu from the Last Supper. *What is this thing? MONET? His personal, handwritten journal? Stuck in the wall of a derelict building in the BRONX? Is this the Dead Sea Scrolls of impressionist art? Or a hoax? Or a joke, like one of the hipsters in the art collective is hosing the old guy? What the hell is it doing in MY HAND?*

He opened the book an inch. He saw scrawled notes in French and pencil sketches. He closed it back up, then examined the spine. Sewn binding, no cracks. As slowly as he could, he opened it to a random deckle-edged page. He saw a sketch of a baseball player – a Yankees outfielder – in an old-fashioned, baggy wool uniform, leaning against a giant Monet haystack. In the distance, barely discernable, Mel could see the outfield fence. He squinted. Instead of billboards for Calvert Blended Whiskey, Gem Blades and Yoo-Hoo Chocolate Drink, he saw…gulp…*water lilies.*

Water lilies. Monet water lilies. Behind a Monet haystack. Next to a player in Yankee pinstripes. Mel thought of that Churchill quote – about the most exhilarating experience in life is being shot at and missed. He felt that now. *You want a piece of me, Satan? Ya got me fired, divorced, kicked in the shins by five-year-olds, ignored by snooty art world gatekeepers, tasered, and evicted. None of that worked, so now you're trying to smack my gob into cardiac arrest. Consider my gob smacked to a fare-thee-well, but I AM STILL HERE. Game on, pitchfork-boy!*

Finally, the day was complete. Mel collapsed on the futon, stretched out and tumbled down an infinite black hole of blissful, dreamless non-being.

CHAPTER NINE

October 4

Mel slumbered a solid fourteen hours. He'd have slept a half dozen more if Sam Dollar hadn't shaken him awake. Sam found him by tracing Velocity via her long-suffering grandfather. Now it was 4 p.m., and Mel was sitting in Velocity's Love Shack art studio in the cracked bucket seat of a 1968 Pontiac Trans Am.

The paintings he'd found – fourteen of them, and three dozen-plus sketches – were spread out on the floor of the studio. They were anchored by assorted door handles, chrome dingbats, and hood ornaments from 1950s American luxury cars. Velocity and Demolition were staring down at them. What was this stuff, and where did it come from?

Velocity's studio was an astonishment: a mini-blimp hangar gouged out of the Ziegler-Haversham Grand Ballroom. Now it sheltered Velocity's towering tribute to the last moment of Eisenhower/Ozzie Nelson American cultural hegemony: tail-fins-and-ventiports kinetic sculptures welded from forsaken Motor City dreamboats of the 1950s. This girl was an ARTIST, thought Mel – the creative progeny of Alexander Calder and Harley Earl, with a touch of Cubist Picasso and Chris Burden tossed in. Her most advanced work-in-progress was a pair of intertwined twenty-two-foot Rock 'Em-Sock 'Em Robots conjured from a '57 Chevy convertible, a '54 Cadillac El Dorado with those glorious Dagmar chrome bumper shells, and a '58 "Torqueflite" Plymouth Fury with directional stabilizer fins. He thought he also saw some wide-track Pontiac quad headlights and the Raymond Loewy bullet-nose from the '51 Studebaker. Awesome.

"So, what do we think we think?" said Velocity, pointing to the art on her cement slab floor.

Mel pried himself out of the Trans Am bucket. "The journal – from what I've read, which is not much – tells us he did all this around 1921. Look at this stuff – what do you notice?"

"Well, let's see," said Demolition. "The colors: basic. Grab-your-eyeballs bright."

"Good," said Mel. "Monet had cataracts. He had to use the most vivid colors to simplify his task."

"So does that mean…you think this is the real deal?" said Demo.

"I don't know what to think," said Mel. "Finding this stuff here makes absolutely no sense, but who would fake this up?"

"Let's say it is real," said Velocity. "How much is it worth?"

"The last major Monet to sell at auction," said Sam, "was 'Nympheas,' the 1908 water lilies. Fifty-seven-point-three million dollars." As one, the group turned toward the patchwork of canvases on the floor.

"Uh huh. Okay, let's round it off," said Velocity quietly. "Fifty million…times fourteen…" No one said a word as everyone did the math. Then everyone had the same thought at the same time: "*I'm…looking…at…seven…hundred…million…dollars. Seven zero zero zero zero zero zero zero zero.*"

"This is the scene in the movie," said Sam, "where each of us wonders how to bump the others off so we can have all this for ourselves."

"No need," said Mel. "This stuff belongs to all of us. I found it in your place. Enough here for everyone."

"If there's anything for anyone," said Demo. "No way this shit is real,"

"Oh? Why not?" said Mel.

"Okay, so this is supposed to be 1921. Monet was born when, 1850 something?"

"1840. November 14," said Mel. *I didn't even know I knew that.*

"Okay, so the dude was eighty-two. A serious painter for sixty years. Rich and famous for, what, forty years?"

"Famous for fifty, rich for forty," said Mel.

"And in that time – in ALL that time – what was his modus? What did he do that made you love his stuff so much?"

"Easy," said Mel. "His paintings are more natural than the natural world, more real than reality. He was the unchallenged master of revealing the glory that's hiding in plain sight all around us. Getting inside a single ordinary moment – like snow, at dawn on a haystack – and turning it inside out, making us see, really SEE the splendor of the world and making us fall in love with it."

"Exactly. And what did he NEVER do?"

"I give up," said Sam.

"He never once painted something that wasn't there. He painted the real world as he saw it." Demo pointed at the art. "Now look at this stuff. It's crazy. It's like, I don't know, dream art, like he was hired by some crazy baseball fan to paint his fantasies. You don't start doing that when you're 81."

"I'm not sure that's true," said Mel. "I think when you're 81 and you're worth a couple of million francs, you do whatever you want. You build a garden just so you can paint it. You have your workers paint your Japanese bridge thirty times to make it brighter. You stop giving a shit what anyone thinks."

"And Yankee Stadium is clearly something he fell in love with," said Velocity. "Like the cathedrals and that train station and the haystacks and the poplars…"

"Except," said Sam soberly, "the journal says 1921. Yankee Stadium didn't open until 1923. So, Demo is right. He – whoever he was – was painting something that wasn't there."

"Oh," said Velocity. "Uh huh. Yeah. Wow." Her brow furrowed.

"So, the big question is still out there," said Mel. "Is this stuff the real deal?"

"Right!" said Velocity. "We need to figure this out. Sooner the better."

"Any ideas?" said Demo.

"Well, yeah," said Mel. He turned to Sam. "I'm thinking Simon Brittle." Sam pondered a moment, then nodded.

"I know him!" said Velocity. "The old guy. Grampa loves him."

"That's because he's the only art expert in New York with an absolutely fool-proof crap detector," said Mel. "92-year-old free-thinker, but they can't get rid of him, he's too good. Gets all the 'holy mother of God' stuff that comes in the front door."

"Think it's safe to take this to the Met?" asked Velocity. "That place runs on gossip. If this gets out…"

"That's the beauty part," said Mel. "Simon's a pal. I can show it to him, no one's the wiser. He'll take care of us. He can eyeball it and pretty much tell us what we've got."

"There's this other guy," said Velocity. "My pal Edison Ziff. He's the son of the guy who saved this place. He's a pro, and he's got all kinds of gear: chem analysis lab, x-ray, UV blacklight…"

"So how 'bout this," said Mel. "Sounds like Ziff's our man to get this stuff certified if it's real. So, I'll take the haystack, you take everything else. I'll let Simon give me a take on it, you show the rest to Ziff. See if he's interested in getting into the weeds for a real authentication."

"Okay," said Velocity. "What about the journal? I have another pal who lived in France for…"

"That stays with me," said Mel sharply. *Where did that come from?* "Sorry. I mean, ummm, I'm puzzling through it, and I…I just want a chance to figure it out myself."

"Okey-doke," said Velocity, hands up in surrender.

Mel stared down at the paintings. "Either we're looking at the most ambitious – and craziest – project in the history of art forgery," he said, "or we're looking at the greatest discovery in art history."

"What do you think, little buddy?" said Sam.

"I think I just stepped on another banana peel on the low road to enlightenment."

CHAPTER TEN

October 5

Mel often heard journalists call The Metropolitan Museum of Art "a city within a city." It had over two thousand full time employees, plus god knows how many part-timers and volunteers. The Met had a full staff to feed the public, and another (better trained, better paid) staff to serve the administrative heavyweights and their money-giving guests in private dining rooms. It had nine NYFD retirees in its fire department and five dedicated sewer hogs to service the 30 bathrooms, 178 toilets, and 144 urinals. It had a full-timer who did nothing but arrange flowers in the Great Hall every Monday morning.

Mel had his own way of thinking about the Met. He thought of it as the English royal court under Elizabeth I as observed by Shakespeare, only with computers and smartphones. Like the Elizabethan Court, the Met was a cesspool of ambition, betrayal, desperation, romance, and the occasional (metaphorical) beheading.

The place was ruled by a clique of lofty, occasionally benevolent despots huddled around the throne of the Director. They were indifferent to the hordes of disgruntled peasants who actually ran the place.

Just below this clique were the curators: the dukes, earls, viscounts, and barons. They were a colorful caucus of courtiers jockeying for power and prestige. These included entitled, incompetent royal squires; haughty, aggrieved wizards forever planning intrigues; and inspired minions laboring for the greater good of an institution that punished them for their lack of political ambition.

Simon Brittle fell into this latter category. In his sixty-seven-year career at the Met, he had rocketed from "Apprentice Appraiser, Authentication Services" to "Associate Appraiser, Authentication Services." His office was a grubby afterthought tucked under a stairwell, the mutant product of a botched architectural do-over in the 70s that resulted in a number of awkward spaces and half-floors.

Simon Brittle had no cronies amongst the Met Museum penthouse dwellers. He had the institutional visibility of a brass stanchion. The only reason the Met kept him around was because he was incomparable at his job: the best in the world at appraising art in a "blink." The trustees, patrons, directors, and curators *had* to keep the guy around for his legendary "golden gut." He was the only one they trusted to appraise and authenticate the stuff in their personal collections.

He'd saved Met Director Chase Hancock from paying seven million for a brilliantly faked Jackson Pollock drip painting with an unimpeachable (sham) provenance and irresistible backstory. The seller, a Native American art professor from Taos, claimed to have found the painting in a Navajo hogan in Tuba City, Arizona. This is where "Jack the Dripper" had gone to study the sand painting techniques of the tribe's medicine men. Brittle took one glance and told Hancock the spatter patterns were too random. Hancock had it carbon dated. 1961, five years after Pollock died in a car accident.

Hancock thanked him with a five-dollar gift certificate to Dunkin' Donuts, slipped under his office door.

Mel had bonded with Simon Brittle the first moment they'd met back in 1998. Mel had been staring at Edward Hopper's "The Lighthouse at Two Lights" when he heard an excited, raspy voice pipe up behind him. "Whaddaya think, genius?" He turned and stared down into bemused brown eyes set in the gnarled face of a geriatric, emaciated elf.

"I, ummm, like it," Mel stammered. "I mean, it's a, you know, masterpiece."

"That's it?" said Brittle. "C'mon, you're a goddamn painter yourself! You can do better than that! Put your back into it!"

Painter? Mel was clad in his stained one-size-fits-no-one security guard blazer. "What makes you think…"

"Kiddin' me? I see the way you look at the pictures here. Like this one. You been lookin' at that thing for an hour, takin' it apart, scopin' out how Hopper did it." The elf turned his head from Mel to the Hopper painting. "But of course, the real question has gotta be WHY he did it. Painted that lighthouse that way." Back to Mel. "So, tell me whatcha think, genius."

Mel was so surprised by this stranger's benign intrusion that he let down his guard. "I think," he said, then stopped. What *did* he think? I mean, *really* think?

Simon's smile nudged him forward. "Yeah?"

"I think that Hopper…I mean, it's a metaphor, isn't it? For the existential plight of mankind." Whew! *Where did that come from? Oh well, in for a penny…* "It's a kind of epiphany," he continued. "Hopper's telling me that I'm absolutely alone in this world. In fact, I've always been alone, and the idea that I'm not is a children's fairy story I was taught at birth. So, there's the shock of that. And then there's the paradox."

"Paradox?" A smile, and then a nod. "Good. Keep goin'."

"So, Hopper tells me I'm alone by creating a work of popular art that connects me across the world with art lovers everywhere, right? Like the two of us, here, now. There are millions of Hopper lovers who know this secret, and now we're alone together in loving the thing."

The elf cackled. "Nice work, genius. I knew Hopper. Cantankerous old bastard, real misanthrope, but loved to hang out here and watch people ogle his stuff." He stuck out his knobbly hand. "Simon Brittle. Gladda meetcha. You and me? Birds of a feather. We're gonna get along."

No one knew the Met Impressionist collection like Simon. Mel had spent a hundred hours standing in front of Van Gogh's "Wheat Field With Cypresses," but a half hour with Simon proved he'd never really seen it. From Simon, Mel learned that…

1) This was the "July 1889" version. The National Gallery in London had the "September 1889" version.

2) Van Gogh completed it just after "Starry Night."

3) The Met had purchased the painting in 1993 for 57 million dollars.

4) It might be Van Gogh's work, or it might be a masterfully-done forgery.

That last bombshell caused Mel's jaw to bounce off the marble flooring. He stood enraptured as Simon talked about "impacted impasto." "Look," said Simon, "Van Gogh coulda painted both versions during his stay at the Saint-Rémy asylum. Then he'd have shipped them in a leaky crate to his brother Theo. The paintings woulda dried, cracked, and crumbled. But this one looks great. Why?"

The first link in the chain of provenance was Emile Schuffenecker, whose brother Amedée was an art dealer. Emile was charged with "restoring" the Saint-Rémy paintings. "He might have copied the "September 1889" painting and sold it as an original," said Simon. "Supposedly painted two months apart, but the skies are the same. Why? Ya gonna tell me Van Gogh painted his own painting instead of what he saw out his window? HA! And who sold it to the Met? Scumbag who peddled guns to the Nazis and took the art they looted as payment."

"So, you're saying…"

"I'm saying I love my job and I don't make waves and it's probably from Van Gogh's hand, but I've just entertained us both for ten minutes. So, I'm starving. You? Gotta place that'll kill ya. You're buyin'"

Besides their shared passion for selected works at the Met – 19th century French Impressionists and 20th century American illustrators – Mel and Simon shared a love for the ham-and-brie-on-onion-brioche sandwich featured in the snooty 4th floor Kravis Wing Members Dining Room. Brittle smuggled Mel up there every Friday at 2 p.m., after the plutocrats had puttered off. Simon loved telling stories about his seven decades at the Met. He'd regale Mel with museum gossip: which curator was banging what intern, which beloved Met patron was about to be busted for running a Ponzi scheme, and which twenty-something tech genius had just paid a Nigerian eBay vendor two million dollars for a laughably fraudulent Warhol soup can.

Best of all were his stories about his crazy mother, "Lolly." Simon described her as "half Georgia O'Keefe, half Zelda Fitzgerald, all Auntie Mame." "One time she told me my father was Picasso," said Simon. "Another time it was Jack Dempsey. Still another it was Charlie Chaplin. Other kids were out playing baseball, I was in the goddamn Louvre getting a lecture from mom on why "Virgin and Chile with St. Anne" was Da Vinci's masterpiece rather than the 'banal' Mona Lisa. By the time I was ten I could tell a Monet from a Manet. I could also make a mean pitcher of bootleg gin martinis for mom and her pals. The truest thing she ever said to me – this was right before she disappeared with her artist boyfriend to drive an ambulance for the Loyalists in the Spanish Civil War, I was fourteen at the time – was 'I did pretty well with you for someone with no maternal instincts whatsoever.'" She was the world's worst mom – I mean, she abandoned me when I was fourteen! – but man, we had a blast. And being on your own at fourteen, in New York, with your own pad and just enough money to get by? That wasn't so bad. Made me get my shit together."

So here was Mel standing outside Simon's door holding an artistic hand grenade: umpteen-million dollars of (maybe) original (perhaps) Monet artwork rolled in a cardboard shipping tube. Why was he hesitating? Simon was the only friend he could trust with this, right? Mel steeled himself, knocked on the door, opened it and walked in. "I've decided to perk up your sorry day with something that I think you'll find very, very..." Mel froze. *What? Oh, shit...*

"Yes?" Simon had morphed into an imperious woman in her late 40s, wearing a grey heather one-button power blazer over a white silk blouse and black pencil skirt. A bleak, tight-lipped half-smile creased an austere face framed by a tightly bound chignon of ebony hair. "What is it? What have you got there?"

Hesitation is death. Turn around and run, NOW.

CHAPTER ELEVEN

Mel didn't run. Instead, he shuffled forward, pulled by the tractor-beam of this woman's autocratic glare. "I, ummm…need to…that is, do you, ummm, know where Simon is?"

"He's out. Old fool twisted his ankle at a tango class, of all things." She stuck out her hand. "Roxanna Wetherley, Interim Consulting Appraiser, Authentication Services. I can help you."

Mel shook her hand as she stared at the tube. "Ummm, Melvin Flack, I'm, uhhh…I work in Security. Guard. Security Guard. I just came down to see if Simon wanted to have lunch…"

Before he knew what was happening, she slid the tube from the crook in his arm and popped off the plastic cap. "Is this something for Simon?"

"NO!" he blurted. *Stay calm.* "That is, I mean, it's…just something…it's nothing…look, I can wait till he comes back."

She started to work the canvas out of the tube. "He's going to be out for at least two weeks. What is this?"

"It's nothing, nothing. Found a bunch of these in a, you know, Salvation Army Thrift Store. Nothing. Look, I'll come back later." He was babbling, his feet nailed to the floor. *Grab the tube, walk out! Do it! NOW!*

"But you thought it was worth having Simon take a look."

"We're pals." Mel attempted a discreet lunge at the tube, but the woman had turned to Simon's ancient taboret art table to spread out the painting. "I, uhhh, really don't want to waste your time with this silly thing…" But she was already smoothing it out, docking the corners with Simon's art deco cherub paperweights. Then she stepped back and took it in. She tried to remain stoic, but her eyes went wide.

"You, ummm, said you found a *bunch* of these?" she asked, the smallest tremor of excitement edging into her voice.

"No. I mean, they were rolled up…"

"Where?"

"Just this funky garage sale…"

"I thought you said thrift store."

"Thrift…that's right, thrift store that, was, ummm, having a garage sale. Look, there's no reason you should be bothered with this thing…"

"Where are the others?"

"You know, back at my place. I'm staying with friends…"

"Have they seen this? Or anyone else?"

"What? No, I just…." He felt clammy, the blood pooling in his feet. *Don't faint.*

"You were right to bring this in. Why don't you leave it overnight, I'll give it a once over."

"Uhhh, no, I'd rather…." He lurched toward the painting, but Roxanna blocked him with a dainty hip bump worthy of a Balinese dancer. She handed him her card.

"I'll do some quick UV light work on it, just to make sure it's nothing. You don't mind, do you? I mean, we're both on the same side here. What's good for the Met…" She pulled out her smartphone and inhaled the work in a clickety-click of digital captures.

He considered his options. He could muscle past her, grab the painting and smartphone and dash out. She'd track him down, get him fired. Damn. "Well, ahhh…"

"Fine. Come by tomorrow, I'll tell you what you've got. You're probably right, it's nothing. Now if you don't mind, I've got a rush appraisal for one of our biggest benefactors…" She frog-marched him across the threshold and slammed the door, bumping him into the hallway.

Something had just happened, but what was it? And what could he do about it, whatever it was? *You can't unmake the soup.* As he walked away, he tried to quell the sense of panic that threatened to plug his throat. He realized he'd stopped breathing. He came to a halt, closed his eyes, and inhaled as deeply as he could. *Let it go. Just another thing I can't do anything about. Global warming, the Mets bullpen, the inevitability of death, a suitcase nuke in Times Square, the possible disappearance of Turner Classic Movies from cable…and now this. Let…it…go.*

CHAPTER TWELVE

October 5, Evening

Mel dreamed of his fantasy living quarters as a teen and evolved that fantasy for four decades. *Greenwich Village, definitely. Privately keyed elevator to a penthouse. Capacious but cozy, with a solarium offering Gershwinesque views of the city, especially at night. Eighteen-foot vaulted ceilings. Art studio on the ground floor, with a cast iron spiral staircase to my loft bedroom snuggled inside a floor to ceiling zillion-book library. And art, of course. Every inch of every wall covered with my own breathtaking originals intermingled with signature works of the world's greatest artists purchased by genius me when those artists were unknowns.*

Mel was now standing in his dream space, his mouth agape as Velocity and Demolition circled around their art booty laid out on the floor of Edison Ziff's studio. Sam Dollar was nearby, staring out the huge windows checking for snipers. This place was so...so...*him*, and so...so...*complete,* as if an architect and interior designer had vacuumed this fantasy from his skull and rendered it as a Broadway stage set. Vaulted ceiling, solarium, spiral staircase, loft, shambolic workspace, art-covered walls: about two billion dollars' worth, reckoned Mel. *Where did he get this stuff?* The 20th century wall featured vivid original work interspersed with paintings by Willem de Kooning, Pollock, Picasso, and Edward Hopper's "New York Movie" with that lonely blonde usher. The opposite wall? Degas, Vermeer, Seurat, Cezanne, Renoir, and Monet: specifically, his "Rouen Cathedral, Effect of Morning." The kitchen featured garish film noir posters from the 1940s: "I Wake Up Screaming," "Stranger on the

Third Floor," and the French poster for "Lady from Shanghai." And this place went his fantasy one better. Of course! A red and gold neon Wurlitzer 1015 "Bubbler" jukebox played raunchy rhythm and blues hits from the 1940s, like "King Size Papa" by Julia Lee.

Ziff himself was roughly Mel's age but seemed twenty years younger because of his furious vitality. Bald head with a pewter ponytail, navy sport jacket over a gray paint-spattered long-sleeved tee, and blue skinny jeans. He put his arm around Mel as Mel stared at his wall of art. "Ed Ziff. And you must be…"

"Melvin Flack." Mel nodded toward Ziff's Monet cathedral. "How'd you get your hands on that?"

"Easy," said Ziff. "I painted it myself."

Mel's mouth fell open. "That? It's a…"

"Fake!" said Ziff. He shot his index finger at every painting on both walls. "Fake, fake, fake, fake, fake, fake." His raspy laughter boomed through the loft.

"Wow. They're so well done. Nearly perfect," said Mel.

"They are not nearly perfect, my friend. They're *absolutely* perfect," said Ziff, grinning. "They *have* to be perfect. I know because I painted them. That's the only way I can send up this whole idiotic system that rips off artists and makes rich people richer." He dragged Mel in front of an impeccable fake of Picasso's "Large Still Life with Pedestal Table." "I slipped this into an auction at Christie's, and a Japanese cosmetics magnate bid sixty-one million dollars for it…until someone told him it was an original Edison Ziff. It's the same damn painting! How come it's not worth the same damn price?"

"Uncle Eddie?" It was Velocity. "We're ready when you are."

"'Kay!" he shouted to Velocity. He smiled at Mel. "Grab some wine. This is gonna be fun."

• • •

The group was properly Merloted as they settled into the sofa and club chairs. Mel described the debacle with Roxanna Wetherley, and then Ziff got to it. "Well, first of all I'd like to congratulate the group for doing everything wrong," he said as he stood over the paintings. "Velocity, you of all people should know better."

"Like, what did we do?" said Demolition.

"Like, you handled artwork that could be 90 years old with your bare fingers, so the oils in your skin could degrade the paint." He yanked on gloves he'd pulled from the hospital operating room box on his desk. "Powder free nitrile gloves, people. Art Conservation 101."

"That it?" said Velocity.

"Then, of course, rolling the art back up into the damn tube? So the paint could crack, chip, flake, and peel just a little more? The only smart thing you did was bring it here so I could save it before it crumbled completely."

"So, you've looked at 'em, right?" said Velocity.

"Yeah, I've looked at them."

"Whaddaya think?" asked Sam Dollar.

Edison Ziff cast his gaze downward. "Let me tell you what I know. Then I'll tell you what I think."

"Okay," said Mel.

Once again Ziff paused, gathering his thoughts. "Here's what I know. Eyeballed the state of the canvas, and did some off-the-cuff infrared, X-ray, and UV light work. The impacting and denigration of the impasto is consistent with something done ninety years ago, then rolled up and stored in the wall of a building that was hot-humid in the summer and freezing cold in the winter. And whoever did this knew a helluva lot about the work of our friend Monsieur Monet: his palette, his brushwork, his sense of composition." Mel felt the hair on the back of his neck prickle to attention.

"So, what do you *think*?" asked Velocity.

"I've studied Monet." Ziff pointed to the mock Monets on his wall. "Took me two years of practice before I could paint with his hand, using his palette." Ziff looked directly at Velocity. "I think – can't prove, but I think – that everything here was painted by Monsieur Monet."

A hush. Velocity looked at Demo. Sam looked at Ziff. Then everyone looked at Mel, who gulped and then stammered, "Really? What makes you…"

"Three things," said Ziff. "First, the scope of the fingerprint. I know his late palette because I used it when I was faking his work. Very specific. Vermillion. Toluidine red. Pale cadmium yellow, cobalt blue, and emerald green. Small number of vivid colors. The man was going blind. He needed that, whaddayacallit... *bigness*. I X-rayed the canvas. He built these paintings the way he built all his work at Giverny. The architectural under-sketch, the composition, the brushstrokes, the signature: Monet, Monet, Monet, Monet."

"So, what's thing number two?"

"The zaniness of the subject matter says Monet."

"How does..." began Sam Dollar.

"Think about it," said Ziff. "Think about the ambition of this project, the amount of work the artist put in. Now imagine yourself back into the 1920s. You're an ambitious art forger desperate to make a sale to a gullible millionaire. Are you gonna spend three years doing some off-the-wall shit like this? Or are you gonna copy something right from the heart of the Monet canon: haystacks, cathedrals, the Giverny gardens? You want something that a wealthy sucker is going to assume is by Monet, because it's so goddamn Monet-like. These aren't. They're too weird not to be real."

"Makes sense, I guess," said Demolition. "What's number three?"

"The lost summer of 1921," said Ziff. All four wrinkled their brows, arched their eyebrows, and cocked their heads at the same time. "In the spring of 1921, Monet's friend Georges Clemenceau came to Giverny to give his friend Claude some bad news. When he was President of France, Clemenceau convinced the French Parliament to pay for a dedicated Monet Museum, a kind of mini-Louvre just for the great man's work. Monet, naturally, was over the moon. This was something that would live beyond him, where art lovers would come for a thousand years to fall in love with work from every phase of his life."

"Then something went horribly, horribly wrong," said Velocity.

"How did you know that?" smiled Ziff.

"Because of how you're telling this story."

"You're right. Clemenceau left office in 1920, and Parliament cancelled the museum funds. I mean, France was underwater trying to pay off World War I. So here was Monet, his great dream in ruins, spurned by the country he'd spent his life glorifying. I've read his journals. He was outraged. Heartbroken." Ziff paused, opened his mouth, then stopped.

"And?" said Demolition.

"And then…nothing. Nothing for the summer and fall of 1921. This is a man who never stopped sketching, never stopped painting, never stopped journaling, never stopped writing letters to his thousands of friends around the world. Suddenly, zilch. No paintings, no journal entries, no letters. No record of Monet visiting the eye doctor for his cataracts. No dinner parties, no auctions of his work, no special exhibitions." He smiled and looked at Mel. "Where was our genius friend?"

Mel gulped. "Ummm…the Bronx? Maybe?"

"I don't know that he wasn't," said Ziff. "Of course, there's no record of his being here, either. I mean, New York had twelve newspapers putting out five editions a day, you can't tell me they'd have missed a visit from a world-famous artist like Monet."

"He could have gone anywhere," said Velocity. "He loved painting London. And the seashore. He could have painted some more cathedrals. Why would he come here?"

"Yeah, to paint something that didn't exist?" said Sam Dollar.

Demolition turned to Mel. "How's the Journal coming?"

"Slow, but I'm pretty sure it's in there."

"Before everyone gets too excited, this still could be a hoax. Some millionaire's prank gone wrong," said Ziff.

"But that's not what you think," said Mel.

"No," said Ziff. "I think this stuff is the real deal." He turned to Mel. "So if it is, are you ready?"

"For what?"

"You're about to become a celebrity. And rich."

"The stuff belongs to all of us," said Mel, opening his arms to the group.

"But you're the big story, Mel. Security guard stumbles on pot of gold, luckiest man alive, blah blah blah. Get your umbrella, a shit storm is on its way."

"Shit-storm?" said Mel uneasily.

Ziff snorted. "Think I'm kidding? Google 'lottery winners, comma, suicide.' You are about to be hurled into the mosh pit of the twenty-four-hour novelty-hungry news cycle."

"Dude, that's stark," said Demolition.

"Hey, it's not all bad," said Ziff. "You *will* get invited to nice parties and have your picture taken with Holcombe Parkes. And you'll get a featured obit in the New York Times."

CHAPTER THIRTEEN

Midnight.

Mel's forehead throbbed as he struggled to finish translating another passage from this damn journal. He was encircled by the "Larousse French-English English-French Dictionary," "The Big Blue Book of 555 Fully Conjugated French Verbs," and "Lightning-Fast French for Clueless Beginners." He gazed at the scrawled passage:

"Toujours les mêmes questions, jour après jour, quand j'étais un gamin de 22 et meaintenant comme un ronction de sénescence au 82. Pour ce que je suis prêt à jouer ma vie, saigner, frapper contre ma tête contre, et être complètement déraisonnable? Quelle impossible que je réalisai, ou mourir en essayant? Mes deux amis sinistres me saluent chaque matin - la peur et l'indolence. On lui promet l'effacement, l'autre la stupeur de l'oisiveté. Heureusement, je sais que Dieu cache les peines de l'enfer dans la promesse du paradis. Travaillez, flemmard! Se levez, feignasse! Il ne se termine jamais. Il ne tourne jamais correctement. Il ne devient jamais plus facile, seulement et toujours plus difficile.L'énigme de l'ambition insensée ne peut jamais être résolu. Heureusement, la contemplation productive furieuse de cette énigme à l'aube dans mon jardin se traduire par de la lumière dans l'art est métamorphique, révélant une vision du divin - pas la capture, juste la vision elle-même. Cela doit suffit."

He could barely read his own hen-scratch with its false starts, cross-outs, and substitutions but when he did, he felt giddy. He'd done it! Damn! Beyond the accomplishment of converting the language, there was a thrilling sense of connecting with the man himself. Monet poured out his struggles in the simple, direct way only a fellow artist could understand:

"Always the same questions, day in, day out, when I was a cub of 22 and now as a senescent codger of 82. What am I willing to stake my life on, bleed for, bash my head against, and be completely unreasonable about? What impossible thing will I achieve, or die trying? My two sinister friends greet me each and every morning – fear and indolence. One promises obliteration, the other the stupor of idleness. Fortunately, I know that God hides the punishments of hell in the promise of paradise. Work, lazybones! Get up, slugabed! See! Sketch! Paint! It never ends. It never turns out right. It never gets easier, only and always more difficult. The riddle of senseless ambition can never be solved. Fortunately, the furious, productive contemplation of that riddle at dawn in my garden translating light into art is metamorphic, revealing a vision of the divine – not the capturing, just the vision itself. That must suffice."

Mel had the eeriest feeling: that these words were written just for him, that Monet was reaching across time to cleave the frozen carcass of Mel's artistic soul and let in some light. *My god*, thought Mel. *Monet! Claude Monet! He felt exactly like I did when I gave up. He felt hopeless, but he never quit, the bastard.* Only then did he realize that hot tears were streaming down his face, and he was gulping air. He was right to think creating art is an impossible task, but…well…what if he was dead wrong to use that as an excuse to give up?

Mel was in the bathroom preparing for another night of staring at the ceiling. As he flossed, he did the math in his head for the umpteenth time. Fourteen paintings, about forty sketches, and the journal. Forty million a painting? Fifty? Whole lotta tech billionaires and Chinese real estate kingpins out there. Who's to say each Flack Monet might not fetch *eighty* million dollars? Or a *cool hundred?* At a hundred million, that's one point four *billion* dollars. *Billion with a B. This could actually happen. Divided by however many Moist Robots get cut in, I'm still going to be rich beyond my wildest dreams. What would that be like?*

Mel looked in the bathroom mirror. He was accustomed to Loser Man looking back. Pete Best. Wally Pipp. Was this now the face of a *multi-millionaire*? What would he do with all this money? His brain lit up with a crazy, random cascade of images, ideas, and fantasies.

An art foundation of course. The M. Durward Flack Racially Diverse Foundation for Properly Worshipful Young Female Acolytes.

And a Porsche. Not a new one, but his dream car, the butterscotch "bathtub" Porsche 356 convertible that Steve McQueen's knockout girlfriend drove in *Bullitt.* Wow.

And a Manhattan penthouse studio like Edison Ziff's. In fact, why not just hand Ziff a blank check so Mel could move into that very studio?

Plus, a rustic summer studio in Vermont in a converted barn.

And an oceanfront condo in Kauai.

And a modest private jet – nothing showy, just a, you know, Gulfstream G450, maybe even "gently used" – so he could oversee his empire with regal grace, free from the indignity of the middle seat.

And what about a nationwide chain of art galleries attached to organic, gluten-free, vegan restaurants where homeless people would only pay what they could afford, and upper-middle-class art lovers could feel really *good* about stuffing themselves on sea-urchin tongues, pickled kelp and foie gras? And then they could splurge on an original Flack for dessert! And the proceeds would support his Art Foundation, like Paul Newman's salad dressing empire!

And since he'd be famous and the demand for his work would skyrocket, Mel might have to create a kind of innovative "art factory" like Rembrandt and Keith Haring. He'd hire the best students from his Foundation and have them "complete" the paintings he "envisioned." And these paintings could then be sold at his chain of art galleries! Flack-branded, affordable, elegant, and adjacent to the local Trader Joe's. Not like that gawdawful hackalicious schlockmeister Thomas Kinkade, but *classy*. Like Apple Stores.

The world-famous billionaire is about to sleep on the floor again. He rummaged through the tackle box for tonight's beddy-bye cocktail: an Ambien, two Ibuprofens, and half a Xanax washed down with a healthy gulp of Nyquil. Then he collapsed in a recumbent tangle of limbs.

A surprising thought – shocking, actually – popped into his head. *All that stuff I've wanted my whole life…my fantasy shopping list…now that I can reach out and grab it, do I really want it? Any of it?* Picasso's quote flashed in his mind: *"I'd like to live as a poor man with lots of money."*

He thought of Monet's journal, how the great man lived to paint: just that, and nothing else. Yes, he *could* buy the Hawaiian condo and a big-screen TV. He could even buy the 1954 Mickey Mantle Dan-Dee Potato Chips baseball card his uncle had given him and his mother had thrown out, now worth eight thousand dollars. *Or…*he could bypass ten years of profligate affluenza and use his millions to gift himself with what he'd wanted since he was sixteen: *time to paint. Freedom to fail. Time to find out what I'm willing to stake my life on, bleed for, bash my head against, and be completely unreasonable about.* Time, yes. In a t-shirt and chinos in a rented flat with a futon on the floor.

Oh, and the Porsche. Ragtop. He deserved *one* ridiculous toy, didn't he? Yes, he most certainly did.

CHAPTER FOURTEEN

October 6

CRASH. KA-BOOM. BANGBANGBANG.

Huh? *What the hell?*

Mel sat bolt upright, blitzed out of a dead sleep…or was it a nightmare? A wild pack of beefy jet-black super mutants with obsidian durasteel bullet-heads thundered toward him as sirens and bullhorns blasted the air. Without thinking, he rolled sideways onto the sacred journal and stuffed it down the boxers inside his sweatpants.

BANG!! A hideous scorch of sun-bright light blinded Mel as a concussive blast shattered his eardrums. The sulfur stench burned his throat as the mutants jerked him up and dragged him out of the penthouse down the stairs toward their, what, spacecraft?

His snow-blindness gave way to a riot of colors and shapes as the mutants marched him downstairs into a torrent of panicked refugees. Seemed every Moist Robot in the building was getting the bum's rush. Fire? Bomb scare? Pitch black outside, why now? Mel's mind raced. *Oh shit*, he thought. *The last remaining original Flack, "Garden Bride, Queens" was still up there.* He wrenched his body around to sprint upstairs, but the robocops crushed his arms as they spun him back. Mel bicycled his legs just enough to keep pace with the surging breakers of bohemian humanity cascading out the front door into the street.

Mel bounced off the pavement and landed between a pair of equally dazed MRs. A paunchy young man in spattered overalls was still holding a can of green Krylon spray paint. A skinny female in a "More Issues Than Vogue" t-shirt was sprawled on top of her smashed laptop. Both righted themselves and swiveled their heads, trying to figure out how they got here and what to do next.

Mel sat up and did a body scan. The heels of both hands were crosshatched with blood and grit from breaking his fall to the pavement, but that seemed the only damage. He was clad in what he'd slept in: Sam's NRA t-shirt, Gap sweatpants, and clompy work shoes. Monet journal? Check, stuffed in his undies. He twisted around, shook out the cobwebs, and saw Velocity. What was she doing? Watching something.

Mel jogged toward her and saw what she saw. Three figures stood in front of a periwinkle blue satellite news truck screaming "NEWSBREAKERS LIVE!" The first was a microphone-wielding Brenda Starr in a short sleeve black spandex mini-dress. The second was her buzz cut, blocky cameraman aiming the key light of his shoulder-mounted live shot camera at the third figure, the centerpiece of this event. And this was…Mel blinked and felt the acid backwash of last night's lasagna gargle up in his throat. *Oh shit. Couldn't be.* But it was. Rat-faced Holcombe Parkes, sporting his signature scruffy toupee. He was grinning like a Blaster Blender pitchman as he pointed to a huge, garish piece of concept art.

. . .

Mel came up on Velocity. "Are you okay? I…"

"Sshhhhhhh," she whispered, and turned him toward the NEWS that was breaking LIVE for everyone in the New York metroplex. Mel listened.

"…gotten rumors that a bunch of squatters were trashing the site of my newest project." Parkes was full of bluster, as usual. "I said enough's enough, time to take out the trash!"

NewsBarbie turned toward the camera and walked three steps to her right, so the camera could capture the police drill. "And that supervised evacuation is what you're seeing live, right behind me."

Parkes shuffled with her to stay in the shot. "Burned-out losers, gotta be a meth lab in there. These people are scum."

"Nice," murmured Velocity.

"Pots and kettles," said Mel.

They both turned back to the concept art. "And this had to be done so you could move ahead…"

"…with a project that is gonna wake up the city that never sleeps!" Parkes grinned, then leaned over to her and stage-whispered, "This is kinda top secret, but…"

"Tell us!" squealed the reporter.

"Okay. Property we're standing on? Mine as of one minute after midnight this morning. And very soon it's going to be the new 'Parkes Place' Impressionist Art Palace and Hotel-Casino Plus Luxury Condos. Twenty-three hundred and forty one construction jobs!" Parkes gave the camera two thumbs-up. "It's gonna create what I'm calling a 'Bronx Parkes-perity Zone,' six blocks in every direction, turning this whole borough into a money-spinner that will make Manhattan look to its laurels."

"The rumor is that you bought this place because of something they found inside it. True?" said the reporter. The bottom fell out of Mel's stomach. *Couldn't be…*

"Whoa, you're gooooood!" She grinned as Holcombe smirked. "What got found was…well, let's call them 'assets,'" said Parkes. He turned to the camera lens. "No, my friends, let's call them what they really are: astonishing, one-of-a-kind treasures that are gonna stun the world. Right here inside a wall in this crummy building. These treasures are like…like…" He seemed to search for a colossal enough comparison. "Tut's tomb meets the Titanic!" Back to the reporter. "Stuff's gonna get millions of tourists from all over the world to come here to book hotel rooms, to spend money, to have the time of their lives!"

"Oh shit," said Mel. *Damn you to the lowest rung of hell, Roxanna Wetherly.*

The perky news babe turned to the camera. "From anyone else, that might sound like so much wishful thinking. But from Holcombe Parkes, the Mad Midas of Manhattan, well, you can believe it!"

Parkes leaned into the camera for a last bite of the apple. "In fact, you can take it to the bank. Because," he chortled, "That's sure what I'm gonna do!"

The reporter tossed it back to the newsroom and the camera guy killed the sun gun. Holcombe allowed himself an exuberant Tiger Woods fist pump and walked back toward his luxury SUV.

Mel was enraged. "Hey! Hey Parkes!" Parkes stopped but didn't turn around. Mel could see a cluster of power-suited henchmen scurrying toward them. "What the hell is going on? Like you couldn't have waited till sun up? Let these great kids gather their artwork and stuff..."

Parkes wheeled on Mel and sneered, "Who are you, little man?"

Mel's momentum caused him to bump Parkes in the chest. He backed up a step and said, "I, sir, am Melvin Flack, and these are my friends..."

Before he could finish, one of the troopers knifed in front of his boss and began backing Mel up, using his index finger as a prod. "Melvin Durward Flack? Well, well. So happy you've saved us the bother of hunting you down."

"What do you..."

Legal Boy produced a business card and flashed it in Mel's face. "Nicholas Dunworthy Junior, of Dunworthy, Natwick, Chandler, and Blake." He opened his leather folio and pulled out some papers. "Your friends can witness my serving you this notarized document demanding that you produce within forty-eight hours property allegedly discovered by yourself inside the Ziegler-Haversham Building which is now owned by Mister Holcombe Parkes. This includes works created by one Claude Oscar Monet." The young lawyer handed Mel the document.

"Not so fast." Velocity grabbed the papers from his hand. She scanned them, paying particular attention to the final page of signatures and notary stamps. She looked up at the cub lawyer. "You didn't own the property when the stuff got found. And now you demand we produce this artwork?" said Velocity. "Who is 'we,' Counselor?"

"This is a legally notarized document giving us the authority…."

"WHO is giving you this so-called authority?" Mel smiled. His friend Velocity was up in Legal Boy's face. "Who has decided who owns these works of art? A court? A judge? Can you show me what judge authorized you to make this demand?"

"As owner of this building, Mr. Parkes…"

"What Judge? Because without court authority, you've got a big fistful of bluffing bullshit and you know it."

Mel saw beads of flop sweat form on Junior's brow. "You are trespassing on Mr. Parkes's property…"

"We're on a public street," said Velocity.

"We are fully authorized to demand that you return Mr. Parkes's property…"

"Who said it's his? Authorized by whom?" pressed Velocity. "Tell me. It's a simple question."

Parkes had had enough. Time to bail out the rookie. He walked toward Velocity. "Listen, cutie, I'll make it simple. I want my pictures. We can yak about judges and legal authority and all that happy horse shit all day long, but I'm the guy who just got the cops to put your shit in the street at zero dark thirty, and if Marvin here doesn't do just what I want I'm gonna squash him – and you – like roaches." He smirked, turned, and strode off, leading a parade of minions back to his trio of gold Escalades.

Demolition appeared from nowhere, with a satchel of goodies. "Your masterpiece," he said to Mel, handing him a canvas with a rubber band around it. "And this is all I could salvage before the hell-hounds chased me off." He gave Velocity a tote bag with five well-loved sketch notebooks. "I hid in a bathroom. They couldn't see shit through those helmet visors. Sorry I didn't get more."

She threw her arms around him and kissed him long and hard. "Love this big galoot."

Demo nodded toward Parkes as the Escalades peeled off. "So, what just happened with our good friend Mister G. I. Luvmoney?"

Mel and Velocity took turns explaining, with Velocity summing it up nicely. "Money talks and bullshit walks."

"That would be us," said Mel.

CHAPTER FIFTEEN

"He can't do that to us!" said Demolition, then laughed, cracking up the other two as well. "No, wait, he can. Just did, as a matter of fact. My bad. So, what do we do now?" All three turned their heads toward the Love Shack, encircled by the same riot cops who had thrown them out.

"Well, let's see," said Velocity. "We've got no place to live…"

"No laptops," said Demo. "Or smartphones."

"Nothing to wear except what we've got on," said Velocity.

"And no cash," said Mel. "Except for that, we're in great shape."

"Had to leave my gear," said Demolition. "Shit. I would love to blow that sumbitch to hell on live TV."

Velocity bent down and unzipped the cargo pocket on her right ankle. "Desperate times call for desperate measures." She pulled out an antique Motorola StarTAC clamshell mobile phone.

"Wow!" said Demolition, laughing. "Velocity gittin' jiggy wid it! Welcome to the 90s! Monica Lewinsky's cellphone, with Bill on speed-dial!"

"Grampa gave me this a couple of years ago in case the Martians attack. No clue if it'll work." She flipped it open, booted it up, hit a series of keys and put it next to her ear. "Hello? Hello? Is that you, Grampa?" Pause. "Yeah, it's Vee. You said, ummm, if I ever got into, you know, trouble…" Pause. "No, not *that* kind of trouble. I'm not in jail." Pause. "It's a little hard to explain. Could you swing by the Love Shack and pick us up?" Pause. "Us. Right. Demo and that guy you met in Mallard's office, ummm, Mel Flack." Pause. "Mel Flack. You know, the security guard. The guy who got shot in the chest with that....that's right, him." Pause. "That'd be fine. See you soon." She closed the phone and slipped it back into her emergency pocket. "Take him about an hour. If anybody can help us get our shit back, Grampa can."

"Let's hope," said Demo. All three watched as the same "Cartage by Cheesebrook" private-haul garbage truck that had eaten Mel's life rolled up to the front entrance. Another squat pair of garbage men in lavender overalls got out and put on their gloves.

"Hope our lawyers can beat up Parkes's lawyers," said Mel.

. . .

To his credit, Van Courtland DeWolfe – a man who could drive any car in the world – did not pick them up in a Mercedes, a Porsche Cayenne, or a Bentley Continental GT. He picked them up in his immaculate 1958 coral and black Edsel convertible. "Third car I ever owned, never saw a reason to part with it," he said. "My friends with Mercedes and BMWs are always having their automobiles vandalized. I get invited to sock hops and classic car clubs."

Velocity told her grandfather what had happened, from the discovery of the paintings onward. DeWolfe was peeved that she hadn't told him sooner. He was worried that what might be the art find of the century was in the hands of that "beatnik" Edison Ziff. By the time he dropped Mel off at the Museum for his guard shift, DeWolfe had promised to help them out. What form that help might take was still a mystery.

Mel placed his rolled-up Queens wedding painting in his locker and began to suit up. As he dressed, he gave Sam Dollar the lowdown on the morning's activities. "Shit, little buddy, that's some nasty badness. What's your next move?"

Before Mel could answer, Dwayne Mallard appeared in the doorway. "Mister Flack? My office. Now."

"Social visit?" said Sam.

"You, my friend, are lucky you still have a job. Were it up to me…"

"But it's not up to you, Mallard. Because nothing is up to you," said Sam. "You are just another corporate nothingburger pushing an empty suit through the air."

"That's about all I'm going to…"

Mel stepped between them. He asked Mallard, "Can this wait till I get off work?"

"I said now. Now means now." He looked at Sam Dollar. "And leave your knuckle-dragging sidekick down here." He spun on his heel and jounced away.

"Good luck," said Sam. "Don't take any of his shit and don't give an inch. Mallard is a toad. He needs written approval to blow his nose."

CHAPTER SIXTEEN

Mel stepped into Mallard's office and winced. The place had an overbearing lavender-chamomile odor. What was it? A Duane Reede air freshener, or Mallard's aggressive aftershave? Mallard sat behind his desk and sipped from his Venti Starbucks as he nodded toward Mel. He cocked his head toward the other person in the room. "I believe you've met Ms. Wetherley." Roxanna Wetherley was doing her best to look aloof, which made Mel chuckle.

"Gal pal of the great Holcombe Parkes," said Mel. He turned to her. "Done with my picture?"

"Ahhh," said Mallard. "The picture. I've been advised of a situation that's...well...extraordinary. I've decided that we should..."

"How many of these paintings do you have?" said Roxanna, cutting Mallard out of the conversation.

"None," said Mel. She grimaced and tried again.

"How many of these paintings did you find in that thrift store or yard sale or whatever the hell it was?"

Mel made a mental calculation. *Is it worth lying?* The truth had to come out, but how soon? *What if they already know?*

"Fourteen," said Mel. "And a bunch of sketches." *The journal is mine,* he thought.

"I'm sorry. Did you say...fourteen?" said Roxanna, shocked. *Shit, they didn't know...*

"F-FOURTEEN?" said Mallard. This thing was so far above his pay grade he couldn't see it with the Hubble telescope.

"Where are the other thirteen?" Roxanna couldn't keep the urgency from her voice.

"Ms. Wetherley, please, remember our agreement," said Mallard. He turned to Mel, suddenly buddy-buddy. "That's quite a painting you gave to Ms. Wetherley."

"I didn't give it to her. She took it," said Mel. Mallard looked at Roxanna, who stared at Mel.

"She told me you asked her to look it over."

"Is *that* what she told you?" said Mel, glancing at Roxanna. She stared at him with a look he knew well. *Little man, you're nothing but a busted flush in this poker game. Give up and let the heavyweights fight it out.*

"That's what I told him, yes," said Roxanna.

"She's lying. I was looking for my friend Simon Brittle. I wanted him to give it a quick and discreet once-over," said Mel, "just to make sure it was nothing special."

"Well, it's quite fortunate you found Ms. Wetherley instead." He turned to her. "Ms. Wetherley, would you share your insights about the work in question?"

She walked forward, facing Mallard and showing her back to Mel. "This painting is authentic to the 1920s. The brushwork and palette are the work of someone conversant with the work of Claude Monet. Monsieur Monet, was, of course, a favorite of New York collectors at that time. Even the signature is remarkable for its verisimilitude."

Mallard smiled at her. "Is this, in your opinion, the work of Claude Monet?"

She scoffed. "Certainly not, don't be ridiculous. That said, I can't at this precise moment prove it's a sham. But common sense indicates it's a bold piece of fakery."

"Why is that?" asked Mallard, leading the witness.

"First, the complete lack of provenance. An original, late period Monet with no paper? None? Never seen, never sold? Please. Second, the bizarre subject matter, unlike anything in Monet's oeuvre. Third, the very idea that not one but *fourteen* unknown, uncatalogued, unseen paintings would show up? By a man who is, arguably, the most beloved, collected, and coveted painter in history? At a thrift store? That's…well…idiotic."

"Great!" said Mel, moving between the two of them. "I agree. Let's go down right now and I'll take that worthless piece of junk off your hands. You told me you only wanted to keep it overnight…"

"Mr. Flack!" barked Mallard. "I'm not certain you grasp the gravity of this situation." He stood up and began to pace. "Somehow you have bumbled onto a trove of paintings that could be one of the greatest art frauds in history. Normally this institution would have no interest such a matter. However, your connection to this Museum changes everything. If it comes out that an employee of the Metropolitan Museum of Art, even a lowly security guard…"

"Thanks for that," said Mel.

Mallard rolled his eyes and soldiered on. "…were in possession of certain fraudulent artworks, and – worse – said employee tried to peddle these artworks through shadowy online auction sources…"

"I have no interest in 'peddling' them," said Mel.

"So you say now. But once those six figure offers start raining down on you? Well, the temptation might be…"

"So, what if I *do* sell them? What's it to you?" Mel and Mallard glared at each other, neither blinking.

"Not me, Mister Flack. US. The Metropolitan Museum of Art. If you were to sell these paintings, the press would go wild. Ten thousand lawyers would start suing you, us, everyone. And the impact on this institution could be catastrophic."

"So why are we here? What do you want?"

"As I know you value your position here," began Mallard with thudding emphasis, "and seeing as how I recently saved your bacon, I'm sure you'll agree the best course of action…" He finally broke eye contact as he smoothed his necktie and sat back down at his desk. "…is to bring in the rest of what you've got and hand it over to Ms. Wetherley."

"*What?*" Mel feigned shock, then outrage. "Why?"

"So she can perform a complete authentication. That puts the institution out in front of this challenge and positions us as the definitive voice in the resolution of what could become a contentious cultural conversation."

"What if they're the real deal?" said Mel. "What then?"

Mallard pushed papers around his desk. "Then this institution will have a conversation with you about next steps, beginning with the fact that the city of New York owned that building by default, and therefore everything inside its walls." He finally looked up at Mel and flashed a fake smile. "So, how soon can you bring them in?"

"Never," said Mel without thinking. He surprised himself. He had a feisty side. Who knew?

Mallard stared at him for a long moment. "Never?" Mel stared back at him as Mallard tried to regroup. "I don't...I'm sure I didn't just...did you just say 'never'?"

"That's right, Dwayne. Never." He heard Sam Dollar's voice in his head. *"Good goin', partner."*

"Okay," said Mallard, staring at Mel. He put some steel in his voice. "I'm going to ask my question one more time, and when I ask it, please remember your sad little job depends on giving me the one and only right answer." Mel nodded. "So. Once again. For the second and last time..."

"I'm not handing them over," said Mel. He was starting to enjoy this. He stared at Mallard. Mallard stared back, then turned to Roxanna.

"Plan B?" said Roxanna.

"Plan B," said Mallard. Then his head hit his desktop with a plonk, and he thumped it three times with his fists.

CHAPTER SEVENTEEN

Chase Hancock was the youngest Director of the Metropolitan Museum of Art in its history. After his nightly double dram of single-malt Scotch Whisky, he indulged in a reverie. His lightning ascension to the throne of thrones at age 38 was an acknowledgement of the radiant white light that emanated from the core of his being: a light that announced to all that they were in the presence of the Chosen One. Upon sobering up, he had to admit that he'd just been damn lucky.

He was named Associate Curator of the Met's Islamic Art Collection right out of grad school at the U. of Chicago in August of 2001. It was his good fortune that his expertise in the decorative arts of the Ilkhanid Period (1256–1353) aligned with the Met's hiccup: a plethora of goodies and a dearth of experts. A month later came 9/11, and the Met decided to sprint toward the crisis rather than away from it. Hancock was trotted out at every PR event, media shindig, and fundraiser for three years in order to brandish the words "understanding," "diversity," "compassion," and "outreach." Chase pivoted from multicultural sock puppet to glad-handing rainmaker. Tipsy prodigal billionaires LOVED this brash, whip-smart, funny young man, and loved tweaking his stuffier counterparts by writing him seven-figure endowment checks.

Hancock fabricated a brash cyber-persona as "visionary museum-maker for the 21st century." Soon he was being featured in "Fast Company," "Wired," and "Business 2.0." He'd unleash his signature quiver of Buzzword Bingo clichés at conferences and cocktail parties, generating awe in tech-doltish Boomers. "Reach beyond the walls…desilo our collections…transform the imperative, and socialize the paradigm until it goes viral." His breakthrough was a 2009 TED Talk where he coined the word that became the title of his cult bestselling e-book, *Emotionation*, a portmanteau of emotion and imagination. "The museum is the last purple place in America," he'd say in his sold-out museum conference seminars, "where red and blue can find illumination through inspiration."

More luck: the position of Director opened up just as the financial calamity of 2008 threw the Met into a panic. The endowment cratered. The ever-dependable source of museum donations – Greatest Generation real estate tycoons and Boomer hedge fund managers – pulled back from giving as they watched their portfolios shrivel. Worse, the art scene flipped in favor of nouveau riche millennial tech billionaires who knew nothing about art history, had no connection with the Met, and treated Great Art as another chip on the roulette table rather than a badge of civic and cultural cachet. Guest surveys revealed that younger people thought museums like the Met were "boring." Why spend a day staring at this old junk when they could spend those hours pinging each other on social media or machine-gunning video game zombies?

Chase Hancock dry-washed his hands as he observed this institutional freak-out. Crisis? Opportunity. He put himself forward as the only person who "got it." He got how to "viralize" the museum, make it relevant to young people. He got how to reach out to snotty tech billionaires and show them how donating their art to the Met gave them a righteous way to one-up their peers. And he got how to do this without pissing off the geriatric core of money-giving trustees, benefactors, and patrons who looked on these new generations of collectors and guests as scruffy, ignorant barbarians.

Hancock won the job. And he *loved* the job. He loved the smarmy, fake adulation of his older donors, who regarded him as an idiot savant mascot. He loved the ridiculously opulent office, fit for the Senior Partner of a heavy-hitting law firm. And, oh, how he loved all that wonderful *money*.

He was smart enough to know what they said behind his back: that he was brilliant but shallow, a mile wide and an inch deep, and certainly – to the older patrons – "not one of *us*." This was code for, "he's new money, non-Ivy League, and *gay*, for goodness sakes. I mean, red sport coats with skinny jeans? And no socks?" But they'd pretend to love him as long as he raked in the megabucks and attracted the new audience. Oh, and the endowment. Had to keep that arrow pointed UP UP UP, baby.

Which is why he was so eager to smother this latest conflagration. *This is your sweet spot*, he reminded himself. *You were put on earth to unknot the problems of cranky, egomaniacal billionaires.* And with that, Chase Hancock welcomed his three guests.

. . .

Mel was dazzled, and intimidated. The place was everything that Mallard's office wasn't: a huge vault of dark oak and marble filled with the sweet smell of centuries-old leather books and perfectly loved antiquities. Here was Very Old Money, Very Well Spent. A cathedral ceiling! A walk-in Citizen Kane fireplace! A Gutenberg Bible! The mammoth first edition of Audubon's "Birds of America" that had sold for eight million dollars just two years ago! Mel was finding it hard to breathe.

He felt a ball of anxiety inflate in his chest. He wasn't worthy to be here. This feeling dissolved as a smiling Chase Hancock welcomed him. Hancock looked like the Creative Director of a hipster ad agency: slim denims, blue plaid shirt under a burgundy cardigan, leather sneakers. He gave Mel a Bill Clinton handshake: direct eye contact, firm grip, and a simple two-pump shake with the right hand as the left embraced Mel's forearm. "So happy you could join us, Mr. Flack. Can I get you anything? Sparkling water, coffee, a soft drink?"

"Ummm, no thanks. Well, coffee, yes. No, Coke. Water, that'd be great. Water. Tap. No ice. Thanks." He was babbling as it was, he hardly needed more caffeine. Hancock's assistant, Jeeves's older brother in full butler livery, retreated to fill the order as the three visitors settled into their antique club chairs. *This chair is worth more than I'll make the next ten years*, thought Mel.

Mallard recapped the conversation they'd had in his office, ending with Mel's refusal to fork over the art. Hancock leaned back in his chair. "Let's get something out of the way first. Ms. Wetherley? The paintings?"

"It goes against all logic and every convention of art history," said Roxanna, "but I've run all the tests: infrared, X-ray, ultraviolet, and XRF light. I put it up against the other Monets here at the Met."

"And?"

"And what this man handed me is in Monet's late palette, rendered in Monet's style. Right now I can't prove it didn't come from the hand of Claude Monet."

Mel's mind raced. He looked at Roxanna. "So, what you said back there…"

"I said it was idiotic to think the stuff is real," said Roxanna. "But not impossible."

Mel turned from Roxanna to Hancock. "Either way it's mine. So can I have it back now?"

Hancock smiled. "What is the subject of this museum, Mr. Flack? Is it…art? Culture?"

"I'm thinking this is a trick question," said Mel.

A small grin creased Hancock's face. "Quite so. The obvious answer, and the default choice of most people, is art. Some scholars say we're about the preservation of cultural memory. Both are wrong. The subject of this museum, Mister Flack…is money."

"Money?" said Mel.

"Money. No moolah, no Monets. And if money is indeed the subject of an institution devoted to showcasing the most sublime works of art ever created," said Chase, "we must accept – no, *embrace* – every inherent paradox in this truth. The largest is this. We here at the mighty Met are an egalitarian center for multi-cultural enrichment that grows in the fruitful soil of rapacious, take-no-prisoners, shoot-the-wounded capitalism. Am I right?"

"You're right," said Mel.

"Facing a paradoxical challenge, we must adopt a paradoxical strategy. We must become a machine for turning the very worst aspects of human nature –greed, pride, and egomania – into a place that inspires the very best aspects of humanity: creativity, kindness, and compassion. Which brings us to Holcombe Parkes."

"Mister Greed, Pride, and Egomania," said Mel, taking the crystal tumbler of tap water from Brother of Jeeves.

"Fair enough," said Hancock. "But let me describe the Holcombe Parkes we welcome at this Museum. Mr. Parkes donated fifteen million art-buying, program-supporting dollars to join our Board of Trustees. You will find his name chiseled on a plaque beside our Great Wall staircase as a Benefactor. He is in our Patron Circle. His investment enterprise is a Corporate Sponsor. And finally, Mr. Parkes is Executive Co-Chair of our Christmas Tree Fund."

"I don't see how…" started Mel.

"A bit more to go," said Hancock. "One more thing about our Mr. Parkes. He isn't content with his current status. He seeks immortality."

Mel's mouth went dry. "Immortality?"

"That's right." Chase smiled. Mel noticed the small gold earring in his left lobe. "And his ability to achieve his goal depends on you, my friend."

"It does?"

"It does. I know all about what you found. Congratulations. Your life is about to change."

"For the better, I hope," said Mel.

"Well, that's why we're here, isn't it?" Hancock said brightly. Mallard laughed just a bit too loudly, adding brown-nosing to his list of ineptitudes.

"Just how is it going to change?" asked Mel. Mel was entranced by Hancock. Like all great salespeople, he didn't beg for your affection. He was the coolest guy in the room, and he made you desperate for *him* to like *you*.

"In one of two ways, Mr. Flack. One possibly ruinous, the other redemptive. Let's call these scenarios 'Futile Resistance' and 'Benevolent Cooperation.'"

"Uh huh. I take it 'Futile Resistance' is refusing to give the paintings to Parkes."

Hancock leaned back and grinned. "Exactly so. You'll be separated from this institution, of course. And then Parkes – or rather, his lawyers – will destroy you. Do you have…guessing here…eleven million dollars to fight them off?"

"The stuff is mine," said Mel. "I found it, I…"

"Mel, Mel, Mel," laughed Parkes. "You think that makes any difference?"

"Ummm…"

"Parkes has more lawyers than the rivers of Bolivia have red-bellied piranhas." Chase was his pal, explaining the facts of life. "After they get the paintings – and they won't stop until they get them, trust me – they'll make sure you're destitute. And unemployable. And homeless."

"So, what's Scenario Two? Give up? Get bullied? Get nothing?"

"Ahhh. Scenario Two. Benevolent Cooperation." Parkes's small smile became a grin. The good news, at last! "In this scenario, you sign the document I've got here on my desk. It certifies that you found these works in a building owned by the city of New York and purchased by Mister Parkes. You relinquish any claim to said artworks and designate their provenance to his development company."

"At which time I get jack-shit and that rat bastard puts them in that craptastic casino-condo monstrosity."

"Is that what you think?" said Hancock slyly, fox to chicken.

"What else?" said Mel.

"Can you imagine a scenario where both you and Mr. Parkes get what you want?"

"I…" Mel froze. He tried for a glib dismissal, but Hancock's sincerity stopped him cold. "No, actually. I can't."

"Here's what's going to happen. It's not the perfect outcome, but we think you'll find it satisfactory. Generous, even."

"Shoot," said Mel. "All ears."

"First…" He paused and held up the first document, making Mel wait for it. "…you sign this aforementioned document, ceding what you found to Mister Parkes." Hancock held up another page of cream-colored paper. "Then Parkes signs this document, donating the artwork to the Met. We allow him to make one and only one perfect, acknowledged, licensed replica of each work for the walls of a gallery in his new development."

"Uh huh," said Mel, still wondering what was in this for him.

"Then Mr. Parkes will donate one hundred ten million dollars to this institution to endow the Holcombe Parkes/Claude Monet Discovery Gallery, an engaging new showcase for these astonishing works."

"Okay, good. But…well, you still haven't told me the part where I get what I want."

"That's the third document you'll sign," said Hancock. He sat behind his desk and produced a third piece of cream-colored paper. "Guess who will be our Permanent Curator, after he signs this third document?"

A shiver of shock roared through Mel's body "M-me?"

Hancock nodded. "Melvin Durward Flack. Starting salary? One hundred seventy-five thousand dollars a year. Equal status with our other curators, with one special privilege: the ability to name your own dedicated Chief Security Officer. Who I assume will be Mr. Dollar, as long as he agrees not to tase anyone else."

Mel's mind raced. *A hundred seventy-five big ones? As a full curator?* From the outhouse to the penthouse in one giant leap for mankind….

"And don't forget," said Hancock, practically purring. "Every single young guest who comes here will know you, the man who lived the legend. They'll seek you out, demand you tell them your story. The story of this gallery will be *your* story as much as that of Claude Monet, my friend."

Mel's eyes swiveled to Mallard and Roxanna Wetherley. Their futures depended on his saying yes as much as Mel's. His brain whispered to him. *What a deal! Six-figure salary. Fame. This is the best deal I'll ever get: a dream deal. My last bite of the apple.* He felt weightless, euphoric.

Mel took the deepest breath he could and held it as long as he could to slow himself down. *This solves all my problems. If I play it smart, I can ride this gig to my grave.* Then something tickled the back of his mind. *I've felt this way before. When was it?* He flashed on evil Mr. Potter offering George Bailey that Vice-Presidency of the First Potterville Bank in *It's a Wonderful Life.* Then his mind dove back in on itself…back, back…and he remembered the first time he'd felt this way. He was back in that moment, sitting across from another super-salesman just like Chase Hancock.

CHAPTER EIGHTEEN

August 23, 1985.

Mel was a 27-year-old starving artist, sitting in the plush corner office of Ralston Dalrymple, Chief Creative Officer of Barkley, Flexner, and Dalrymple Advertising Worldwide. He was dressed in a borrowed sport coat, listening to Dalrymple rave about the samples in his portfolio, especially his fine art display ad for the muffin and pastry selection at Zabar's done in the style of Paul Cezanne. Now Dalrymple was offering him a job as a Junior Art Director at eighty-five thousand 1985 dollars a year. Mel was thrilled and – what's the word? – *relieved*. This solved all his problems! His mother would be delighted. His wife would be ecstatic. His fellow starving artist friends would be jealous. If he still wanted to paint, why, that's what weekends are for. Right?

Right?

He said yes, shook Dalrymple's hand. He was sure the ad gig would suffocate the struggling fine artist he once wanted to be. Ha! As if. That artist never gave up haunting his dreams.

The memory vanished, and Mel flashed on the passage from Monet's journal he'd translated the night before. He had an uncanny feeling that Monet was not only speaking to him but *coaching* him: coaxing him forward with his words.

"I've always wished for comfort and a life of ease, but my soul gives me no rest as it makes a different demand: to find its fullest expression, for its own joy. That's how I've come to know what Sisyphus knew. I know my task is

futile, but it makes no difference because the task is mine alone. That's why I turn toward my fear and open myself to divine annihilation every single day. That is why I descend into my private hell of defeat and futility to confront the beast of indolence and slay it with the only weapon I have: my unquenchable desire to channel the infinite music of God's harmonious natural world and capture a single melody for a single moment on canvas. Utterly impossible...and infinitely soul making. Like Sisyphus, I've got a smile on my face as I watch that boulder roll back down to the bottom of the hill so I can begin again, struggle again, fail again."

"Mr. Flack?" Mel snapped out of his mini-fugue state. Chase Hancock was handing him the third document: the one that guaranteed Mel a curatorship. Monet's words looped in his brain:

"I know my task is futile, but it makes no difference because the task is mine alone. That's why I turn toward my fear and open myself to divine annihilation every single day."

"If you have any questions, please ask," said Chase. He'd hooked the fish, and now he was reeling it in. "If you wish to sleep on it, we can accommodate that, but we would appreciate your answer by tomorrow morning."

Futile...no difference...Sisyphus...turn toward fear...the task is mine alone. Mine alone. Mine alone.

Mel had sprinted away from his soul task thirty-six years before. He'd done it again after his one-man art show tanked. Both times he thought he was chloroforming his ambition. Both times he was wrong. And now here he was, about to abandon the task – *the one that is mine alone* – again, for the final time. This time he knew in the marrow of his bones it would be fatal.

"I, uhhh, don't think I need to sleep on it."

"Wonderful," said Hancock. He handed Mel his fat Watermark pen. "Now, if you'd just sign this document all three times at the red arrows..."

"Mr. Hancock?"

"Yes, Melvin?"

"Thank you for this very generous offer. Really. Thanks. But...that is...no, I can't. I'm not going to take the job." Mel saw Hancock's smile melt into bewilderment. His eyebrows arched. "So, if you'll just give me my picture back, I'll be on my way."

"Oh," said Hancock. "Really?" The plush leather crunched as he leaned back and laced his fingers to support his chin. "I'm....well, I'm very surprised by your decision. Shocked. Are you *sure* you don't want to take a night and ponder this a bit more?"

"I'm sure," said Mel.

"Even knowing what's about to happen?"

"You mean Holcombe Parkes setting his flying monkeys on me? So he can pry this trove of goodies from my cold dead fingers?"

Hancock nodded. "Your claim is precarious at best, and...well, you'll never beat his legal team. And if you lose..."

"*When* you lose," said Roxanna.

"When I lose," said Mel, "thank you, Ms. Wetherley – I'll end up living in a cardboard box over a sewer grate. And Parkes will sue me for the box."

"Yes. Quite so. And so..." said Hancock, brow furrowed, "with the odds against you and so much to gain from cooperating, how can you opt for a strategy doomed to failure?"

Mel stared into Hancock's mystified face for almost half a minute. *How indeed?* "You told me that the subject of this museum – a place that I love, that I think of as my home – is money. You know what? No. Little, tiny, insignificant me says no, you're wrong."

"But..."

"The subject of this museum is something a whole lot bigger. It's something money can't buy. Know what that is?"

"Tell us," said a bemused Roxanna.

"Astonishment. Monet had all the money he needed to live like a king by 1900. Did he retire? He worked harder than ever, because astonishing himself with his talent for turning light into art made him happy. Six million people come to the Met every single year to be astonished. And if I let these paintings end up in the hands of a crass asshole like Holcombe Parkes..." He turned to Roxanna Wetherley. "No offense intended." She nodded and waved her hand with a "go on" gesture. "...then I'm telling the world that I've lost my ambition to astonish. That I agree, it's all about the money, and making art doesn't matter. Then I'm nothing but a…but a….I don't know…*moist robot*, with the shriveled soul of an ATM machine. I can't do that. *We* can't do that."

"We?" said Roxanna. "Who is 'we'? You and who else?"

"Claude, of course," said Mel. "For some crazy reason, fate has chosen me to bring his trove of artwork into the world. And I know from the way this has happened that I've got to do this the way he wanted. A new way, a way that makes the work come alive, that fills people with joy. I've got to do this in a way that makes him happy."

"And you know this how?" said Roxanna.

Mel thought of the journal. "He told me."

Hancock, Roxanna, and Mallard all looked at each other. "He did?" said Hancock.

"Yes."

"I see," said Hancock. "Did he tell you how to fend off someone with resources like Holcombe Parkes?" No sarcasm here. Hancock was interested.

"No, but…well, he chose me to find his trove, not Parkes. There must be a reason. So, I'm going to fight."

"And lose," said Mallard.

Mel laughed. "Define 'lose,' Dwayne. If I take Hancock's offer, I win a lifetime of self-loathing by surrendering before the battle's even fought. I'd have to live with those paintings in a Holcombe Parkes casino." Mel shuddered. "If I DON'T take the offer…" He stood up and surveyed the room.

"What?" said Mallard.

"If I don't take the offer," said Mel, seized by a strange sense of exhilaration, "I'll have the consummate pleasure of finally, after fifty-eight miserable years, finally declaring that I am a FUCKING ARTIST, CAPITAL F CAPITAL A, just like my friend and soul-mate Monsieur Monet, with all the blessings that come with that self-designation!"

"Calm down, Mr. Flack," said Hancock.

But Mel was on a roll. "An ARTIST, Mr. Hancock! Holcombe Parkes can evict me twice in a week. He can take my shit and throw it in one of his dumpsters. He might even be able to sic his jackals on me and steal this magnificent artwork. But he won't do it without a fight. Because he can't take what makes me a real human being, Mr. Hancock. I'm here to do what Parkes can't do with all his billions. He's a eunuch at the gangbang, Chase. Me and Claude? We're *artists*, creating for all we're worth, marinating in the rapture of turning nothing into something, right in the middle of the action."

A wave of exhaustion hit Mel. He was done. He looked at Mallard, who was about to open his mouth. "I know. I'm fired! I'll pick up my shit and get out." Then he turned to Roxanna Wetherley. "Tell your boyfriend he's got a fight on his hands." He stepped forward and stuck out his hand to Chase Hancock. "Thanks again for your kind and generous offer. You're a square guy, although I think you're all wet about the money thing. How I wish I could have said yes. But I can't. Claude told me exactly the kind of place he wanted for his artwork, and it ain't a casino. Or even a museum, for that matter."

CHAPTER NINETEEN

Twenty minutes later Melvin Durward Flack was bounding down the Met steps toward the broad swath of sidewalk fronting Fifth Avenue. He was clad in one of Sam Dollar's navy jumpsuits. Monet's journal was nestled in one of the Glock-friendly cargo pockets. The jumpsuit was three sizes too big, and Mel felt like a chemo patient swimming inside of it, but it did provide a socially acceptable alternative to nudity. He had his rolled-up Queens Wedding masterpiece in his left hand, so he shook Sam's hand with his right. "Thanks, buddy."

"You have really fucked up, my brain-damaged amigo."

"Think so?"

Sam grimaced. "Are you shitting me? A hundred and seventy-five big ones per annum? To glad-hand a bunch of goggle-eyed civilians and pose for selfies? And a great big cushy featherbed for your pal Sam in the bargain? And this from a bunch of greedy bastards who wouldn't give you the paprika off their potato salad?"

"True, but...."

"And you turned it down? To, what, let your arty-farty freak flag fly?"

"I don't understand it myself," said Mel. "But it sure felt good."

"I bet it did. Remember that feeling when we're both homeless." Sam bear-hugged him, causing a "whoompf" of air to stovepipe upward as the jumpsuit pruned around Mel's body. "Okay. Gotta get back in there. The booger-eaters are pillaging the gift shop even as I speak. See ya tonight, ya dumb bastard."

· · ·

Catastrophe had its upside. Like most people, Mel had lived his life sandwiched between the brick wall of grief about his past and the battering ram of panic about the future. Now here he was, strolling down Fifth Avenue on a ravishing autumn morning in the New York of poets, lovers, and artists, like himself. He had nowhere to go, nothing to do, and all the time in the world to get there and do it. For this one brief, shining moment he was Steward of the Claude Monet (Possibly) American Art Trust.

How was he going to make a living while he fought off Holcombe Parkes and the state of New York? Barista? Walmart Greeter? Toast Master at Bagel Boy? Maybe he would start a blog about his adventures. After all, he was about to live the Great American Myth: Righteous Little Guy taking on The Man. David v. Goliath. Luke v. Darth. And with Velocity, Sam, and Demo, he had the makings of a ragtag band of crafty, hardscrabble rebels.

A ninja-black Lincoln Navigator the size of a German Tiger Tank screeched to a stop just in front of him, cuing a bellow of taxi horns. Mel stopped, startled. A hulking ex-wrestler in chauffeur livery trotted around the vehicle and opened the back door. "Get in." He wasn't asking. Mel froze, looked around, then shrugged. Why not? Was this anymore idiotic than the rest of his week?

He got in. The Hulk slammed the door after him.

"Mister Flack? Melvin?" She smiled at him as the luxury tank-limo bounced back into traffic: an attractive woman in a black Armani suit. A beautiful woman really, and beautiful in a certain kind of throwback way. What was it? The perfect oval face? The short, blush-blonde hair, with the strawberry highlights and flecks of gold? The self-assured air? No, it's those beautiful blue eyes, he decided. They're smart. They know something. *"Your secret — that you're a male dumbshit faking your way through life — is safe with me. I'll still sleep with you and make the martinis."* She was beautiful like…like those fashion models Mel had loved in those magazines his parents kept on the living room coffee table. Demure, but shrewd and in charge. His favorite centerfolds in the Playboys his dad hid under the rec room couch cushions had that same knowing look.

Nonetheless, Mel was scared. What did this smart, beautiful woman want with *him*? This couldn't be good.

She stuck out her hand. "Daisy Hudnutt-Parkes."

"Parkes?" said Mel, goggle-eyed. *Ohshitohshitohshit….*

"That's right. Why?"

Mel twisted around and yanked the door handle. Whoops! *It opened!* He wasn't locked in, and he was staring at asphalt whizzing by at thirty miles per. "Ummm, nothing, it's just that…just that…"

"What?"

"Look, you're going to kill me, aren't you?"

The woman's eyes widened, and then she burst out laughing. She laughed for almost a minute, so hard she started to hiccup. Finally, she spoke over the shoulder of her chauffeur-assistant. "Burroughs, are we planning to kill Mr. Flack?"

"Not that I know of, Madame," said Burroughs. "Has there been a change of plans?"

"Not yet. Just keep going." She turned back to Mel. "Let me put your mind at ease, Mister Flack. I'm a lawyer. I've served as a court-appointed attorney to the worst scum on the planet…with the exception of my ex-husband, or course."

"Ex? Did you say…so you are the ex…."

"Ex-Mrs. Parkes. That's right. Collateral Damage of the ongoing Holcombe Parkes 'catch and release' program. Currently starring Dolly L'Amour Parkes, retired purveyor of exotic dances and publicity-obsessed nymphomaniac. So, here's what I learned about murder and how to get away with it. Ready?"

"Shoot. I mean…"

"First, IF I wanted to kill you, I would never, ever, pick you up in broad daylight on New York's busiest street in full view of multiple police surveillance cameras, in front of a place where you're known to hundreds of co-workers in a vehicle easily identified as mine with an expert witness in the driver's seat."

"Oh," said Mel. "Hmmm. Right. Yeah."

"Second, *I* would never kill you. We're already linked by my ex-husband. I'd have Burroughs hire a cut-out to find a discreet, dependable service to send someone to do the job."

"They have that?"

"You don't want to know," growled Burroughs over his shoulder.

"On the night of the murder, I'd check into my luxury alibi hotel with a credit card. I'd choose a place with plenty of cameras. I'd eat dinner in the hotel restaurant. I'd tip my waiter 50% and engage the night clerk, the concierge, and the bellboy in witty banter. I'd over-tip them as well."

"And then this hit man would kill me."

She nodded. "Our unknown assassin would wait till you were alone, kidnap you, and put you in the trunk of his stolen vehicle, probably a 1996 Honda. Why a '96 Honda? They're easy to steal. They started making 'smart keys' in '98. He'd then drive you to…to…oh, Burroughs?"

"Yes, Madame?"

"What is the murder capital of New Jersey?"

"This week? Camden."

"Of course, yes, Camden. He'd drive to Camden and park…" She looked at Burroughs again.

"Behind the Gold Key Motel, Madame. The Hookers N' Heroin Hilton."

"Yes. Oodles of DNA from obvious, easily frame-able suspects. Our hit man would then kill you by the fastest, neatest feasible method, which is…ummm…"

"He'd break his neck, ma'am. Fast, quiet. No weapon," said Burroughs.

"Yes. Then he'd dispose of your body in a dumpster, sanitize the vehicle, park it in the long-term lot at Newark Airport, take a bus home and count his tax-free five-figure cash booty."

"You've really put some thought into this," said Mel.

"Call it a hobby. I've eliminated every conceivable way to get caught. No DNA, no eyewitnesses, no connection to the victim, no weapon. You weren't murdered in my hometown, and I have rock solid proof I was somewhere else when the deed took place. The police need evidence. There is none. I have committed the perfect crime."

"Just guessing here. Any of this involve the fantasy homicide of, oh, say, your ex-hubby?"

She chortled dryly, but there wasn't a bit of humor in it. "My fiancé refers to Holcombe Parkes as a piece of shit," said Daisy. "I disagree. I believe that shit would be horrified to be compared to Holcombe Parkes. When Holcombe dies, they're going to have to build an entire new sub-level of Hell just for him. It will have the charm and sincerity of modern Las Vegas."

A magnificent rant. Quite a woman! "Nice flowers," Mel said, nodding toward the generous floral arrangements in the matching bud vases on either side post of the vehicle. "Toad lilies, yes?"

Daisy cocked her head at Mel, surprised. "Very good. You like flowers? Have you ever painted toad lilies?"

Mel started. "Have I…You…why would I…how do you know I'm a painter?"

"Can we talk about this over lunch, Mister Flack?"

CHAPTER TWENTY

Mel figured Daisy was a regular at Café de Flore because only a regular could find the place. He marveled at the way she hustled him through a single unmarked wooden door next to a derelict television repair shop soliciting long-gone brands like Zenith, Philco, and Admiral.

Mel followed her down a dank, moldy concrete passageway into a place that wasn't so much a restaurant as a botanical garden with a French bistro tucked inside. Chiseled and chipped stone tables huddled under red maple shade trees. Gardeners fussed over daylilies, hibiscus, oak leaf hydrangea, and begonias. Sparrows swooped, pranced, and pounced on pastry crumbs. Mel was intoxicated by the heady blend of scents: lilacs, fresh baked goods, and French press coffee. Daisy and Mel sat on mismatched wrought-iron chairs surrounded by rust-pitted Citroen and Gauloises signs circa 1933.

Mel propped his rolled-up canvas against a table leg. A stooped, rail-thin geriatric waiter in black pants, vest, and bow tie welcomed "Madame HP." She ordered in French for the both of them.

Mel got his first real look at Daisy in the late morning sunlight. He guessed she was in her early 30s. Her rosy skin radiated a youthful glow. No makeup, no vanity, no tricks, no knives, no injections, no anguish. She was assertive self-confidence wrapped around a core of serenity. The faint lines around her eyes and mouth were laugh lines, and she wouldn't notice if you noticed.

The waiter delivered two Cafés Noisette, two raspberry almond croissants, and a plate of meringue cookies, then vanished. Daisy took her cup in both hands, sipped her beverage, and looked Mel in the eye. "Okay, your question. I know you're a painter because I'm deeply in love with a friend of yours."

Mel was surprised. "Who?"

"Simon Brittle."

"Simon? How do you know Simon?"

"He's my tango partner down at the Dance Academy. Wolfey introduced us."

"Wolfey." Mel's brain was failing. He only knew one Wolfey, but it couldn't be. "You don't mean...

She gave him a single nod. "Van Courtland DeWolfe. My fiancé. Wolfey never buys art without a nod from Simon. And..." Daisy smiled wryly. "Simon told me you're a painter, Mel."

"But...but he's never..."

"He said you know things about art only a painter could know. He told me you're the saddest of souls, a painter who doesn't paint. He thinks the world of you, goes on and on. His fondest wish is that you'll take up the brush again."

Mel was stunned. "We've had lunch three hundred times. He never told *me* that." Daisy shrugged and bit into her croissant. Mel pondered this as he followed suit. He washed down the flaky wonder with a sip of his rich coffee drink. "How did you know what happened in Hancock's office? Where to find me this morning?"

"You HAVE to try these cookies," she said, holding out a china plate. He bit into one. *Omigod. Delectable.* She saw the dazed look in his eye and laughed. "See? What did I tell you?"

"Wowsers," said Mel. "What is this place? How come I've never..."

"It's private," said Daisy. "Like a club. Invitation-only, created by foodies for foodies. No telephone number, no address, not on a single tourist map, never been reviewed. The only reason they let *me* in is because of Wolfey. Anyway, to answer your question..."

"Please," said Mel, grabbing another cookie.

"Wolfey knows what happens at the Met before it happens. He told me what was going down. I took a shot, camped out in front. If you don't come out, then you've sold your soul for thirty pieces of silver and Holcombe gets the art. If you *do* come out, that means you stood up for yourself and got sacked. Congratulations. I know what Chase offered. That took courage."

"Thanks." *Stop eating the cookies.* He'd left half of one.

"That means you're going to fight. I'd like to help you." The waiter re-filled their coffee cups from a Queen Anne silver coffee pot. Mel took a large, luscious sip. *Help me. She's going to help me. This beautiful woman has descended from some celestial realm to put things right and affirm the sacred principles of cosmic justice.* Whew! He'd achieved peak caffeination. He felt like he could rip out a telephone pole and use it to pick his teeth.

"Why?'

"Purely selfish reasons," she said. "I made Holcombe rich. I did his deals, invested his money, and told him what real estate to buy. I, Lady FrankenParkes, created the monster the world knows today: a wealthy, ego-obsessed dirtbag with the ethical sense of a velociraptor. When he ditched me, he made it his business to screw me out of the hundreds of millions I made for us. Only he defines 'us' as 'him.'"

"So, you want revenge." He bobbled his coffee cup and splashed his jumpsuit. "Shit. I mean, ooops." Daisy instinctively leaned over to him, her face an inch or two from his, and blotted the coffee with her linen napkin. A shock of lust gushed through his body as he inhaled the scent of her perfume…or was that just her sweet, warm skin? She leaned back. He couldn't remember what he'd just said, or where he was.

"Not really," said Daisy.

"Not really what?" said Mel. *Did I just say that? I sound like an idiot.*

She cocked her head. "Not really after revenge. What you asked."

"Right. Yes. Sorry."

"Any bad marriage, it takes two, doesn't it? After the split, I sped-read every self-help book Oprah ever featured. I screamed, cried, pounded pillows, journaled, cried some more. Finally, I asked myself, 'what really happened?' I was vulnerable, he was predatory. I wanted a savior; he wanted a live-in whore with a genius I.Q. For me, he was like the dessert buffet on a luxury cruise ship: way too much of everything that's bad for you. What scares me about him…" She paused.

"What?" said Mel.

"It's the way he fights, Melvin. He's a thug. He always told me, 'Don't be scared of winning ugly.' Meaning forget about the law or what's right or how many people will suffer, just win, no matter what the cost. That was our divorce. He told his lawyers, 'I want it all. Spend what you need, take as long as you want, but burn her to the ground.'"

"Wow."

"You want to know how we met?"

"Sure, I guess."

"Let's get some real food first." She waved the waiter over and rattled off an order in perfect French. He heard the words "fromage," "saucisse," which meant sausage (he thought), and "caviar." Mel prayed she was picking up the check. If not, he'd be washing dishes for a year.

"So, how'd you meet him?" said Mel.

"I was a street lawyer, struggling to pay my bills. We met at a commercial real estate mixer in 2007. He talked about hiring me, mixing business and pleasure, the usual line. I laughed it off. The next week he bursts into my squalid cubicle and asks me to sue the Cathay Merchants Bank in Taiwan for three billion dollars. That's 'billion' with a B. Why? Because they were publicly demanding he pay back the six hundred forty million he borrowed for a golf course/condo resort deal on the Big Island of Hawaii. Remember Hurricane Flossie?"

"Not really." The waiter tried to fill his cup with regular coffee. He was still buzzed on his close encounter with Daisy's face. He put his hand over his cup. Time to slow it down.

"Wasn't that big a deal. Holcombe had just broken ground when Flossie tore the place up. Holcombe's property was on the other side of the island from the worst damage, just got a little flooding, but he claimed that the 'force majeure' clause in his loan contract meant he could keep all the money without building a single unit. The hurricane was an 'act of God,' therefore the Taiwanese were out of luck. Here's where I should have known what I was dealing with. I showed him five ways he could do the project, pay them back, make a huge profit and make everyone happy. He yelled at me. 'That's not the *point*! It's a *freebie*! I've got the money! We're fucking them, and your job is to make sure they stay fucked!'"

Mel flinched. "Nice."

"Yeah. He had the whole scenario worked out. I was hired to sandbag them until they made some disparaging remark about his character, then we'd sue them for three billion dollars, and the litigation would drag out until the Bank gave up and let him keep the six hundred forty million. And that's pretty much what happened." She smiled at him. "Are you horrified?"

"Water is wet, rocks are hard, and Holcombe Parkes is Holcombe Parkes."

Daisy cackled. "Well put."

"So," said Mel, "What made you think this guy was Mister Right? Assuming you did?"

Daisy thought about this as the small plates arrived: a goat cheese pissaladière, blood sausage with onions, smoked salmon and caviar on baked baguette slices, and ham and gruyère crepes. Daisy smiled and nodded, and the cadaverous waiter turned and disappeared again. "Split everything?"

"Sure," said Mel.

Daisy divvied up the goodies as she spoke. "I was 27, with a hundred twenty-seven thousand dollars in student loans. I'd been turned down for a partnership by Delbert, Rathbone, Sizemore, and Greene. I was working for the city defending dumb, guilty bangers with names like MurderMan and The Shank. Then Parkes called." She took a bite of crepe. "Do you know what the fees are on a three-billion-dollar lawsuit specifically designed never to go to trial? The clouds parted, angels sang, and my bank account crawled out from under a rock. Suddenly, I was solvent. Just as suddenly we were dating, and this ridiculous cartoon character was taking me to the swankiest restaurants in New York."

"Ridiculous?"

"See, that's the thing," said Daisy, slathering her salmon-topped baguette toast with caviar, then taking a bite. Gal had an appetite. He liked that. "He called what he did 'swashbuckling.' It was a game to him. We were his merry band of desperados, ripping off the stuffy suits that were sitting on all that wonderful money that was rightfully his. He could be so….charming." She was looking over Mel's shoulder into a dream-movie of her past, nostalgia laced with regret. Suddenly she was back, eyes fixed on Mel. "Do you know what Franklin Roosevelt said about Douglas MacArthur?"

"No. What?" asked Mel.

"'Never underestimate a man who overestimates himself.' I had the self-esteem of a garden slug – I mean, I was defending thrill-kill teens for rent money, with no prospects – and here comes the Tasmanian Devil in a Brooks Brothers suit with the absolute, unshakeable belief that anything that wasn't nailed down was his and if he could pry it up it wasn't nailed down. Me? I was the crowbar. For the first time in my life…" She stopped, looked down, and leaned back in her chair. "Never mind."

"What?" said Mel.

"We're supposed to be talking about you, Melvin. Your case. And here I am, jabbering about, you know…"

"Jabber away," said Mel, stabbing a juicy morsel of blood sausage.

Daisy considered his offer. "I grew up with this ferocious control-freak mother. You know, married too young, buried her ambition, and was determined to fix things by living through her only child. I made straight A's at Harvard Law because she had a high-powered sniper rifle trained on me at all times. With Holcombe, for the first time in my life I was having *fun!* I'd never met anyone like him: a cross between Cirque du Soleil and Al Capone. I figured out his act was a bluff after two weeks. That's when I started doing his thinking for him. Funny thing was, he loved the grift more than he loved making money. If he could bamboozle a banker? Bully someone out of a fortune so the victim *knew* he was being ripped off? That's when he did the happy dance. Which brings us to you."

"I…" But before Mel could say a thing the waiter was handing him a dessert menu. Daisy waved hers away.

"Is Philippe baking? Can he whip up the profiteroles with stracciatella and chocolate sauce for two? And bring us each a double espresso as well." He strode off, and she turned back to him. "So, what's your plan?"

"Plan?" Mel's brow furrowed. *Uh oh....*

"Plan. To hold onto the artwork. You must have a plan if you quit your job."

"Oh! The PLAN!" said Mel. "Right." He gave her a knowing, conspiratorial look. "My plan is to be kidnapped by a fiendishly clever attorney with unique insights into the psychology of the evil billionaire super-villain I'm facing. And then for the two of us to destroy him through our native wit and guile, restoring order in the universe. So far, it's working perfectly."

She smiled. "And failing that?"

"Failing that, I'm going to burn incense and pray that Holcombe's Escalade is crushed by a chunk of plummeting space debris."

The pastries arrived with the espresso. Mel was still enjoying his caffeine jag, so what was the harm of one final dose of go-go juice? And the dessert! Fresh baked cream puffs filled with homemade vanilla bean-scented, chocolate-flecked gelato, topped with bittersweet chocolate. Perfection. Angels wept.

"So," said Daisy, "What do you think?" Her eyes darted toward her dessert.

"I think," said Mel, riding his caffeine high, "that when mankind appears before the Great Father of Glory on Judgment Day, THIS will be the final deciding exhibit." Mel stood, assuming the role of Mankind's Defense Attorney. "Yes, Most High One, we dropped the atom bomb on innocent civilians, melted the icebergs, and annihilated millions of species of flora and fauna through sheer fecklessness, and we just couldn't stop killing each other in idiotic wars and pogroms and genocides, shame on us. BUT, King of Kings and Lord of Lords, *could any other species* use the sentient gifts of creative inspiration to conceive, conjure, and serve up something THIS delicious?" He held up the uneaten half of his dessert. "I rest my case."

Daisy laughed and applauded along with couples at two nearby tables. Mel flushed with embarrassment. *Was I that loud?* "What is that?" she said, pointing to the rolled-up painting leaning against his chair.

"That? Oh. Ummm…that's…"

"Is that one of your paintings?" she said. "Oooooh, can I see it?"

"This isn't just one of my paintings. This is my only remaining painting, thanks to your ex-hubby." She cocked her head, eyebrows arched. "Long story short, I was sub-letting a rent-controlled apartment. Parkes bought out my landlord and dumpsterized my worldly goods. Somehow his goons missed this." Mel rolled off the rubber bands and unfurled it for her.

"Oh! Oh my! Oh dear…" The blood drained from Daisy's astonished face. Was she going to faint?

CHAPTER TWENTY-ONE

Mel was puzzled. Her eyes blinked furiously as they moved from the picture to Mel, then back to the picture. She was hyperventilating. Finally, she turned away and put her face in her hands. Mel got up, let the painting curl up on his chair. He knelt next to her.

"Daisy, are you…I mean, what's wrong? Is there something that upset you? I know it's not that great…"

She grabbed him around the shoulders and pulled him forward in an awkward hug. He resisted by instinct, then eased into the hug, holding her for a good half a minute. Once again, he was staggered by her captivating scent and the warm glow of her delicious skin. He couldn't imagine what he'd done. He finally felt her push back. He picked up the picture and started to roll it up. "I'm sorry…"

"No! No, let me see it again."

"You sure?"

"Please."

He unrolled it for her. It seemed to put her in a hypnotic trance. He was aware that the other bistro patrons were staring at the painting and at Daisy. After another minute, she nodded her head. He rolled it up and sat back down. "What…"

"I…I told you about my mother."

"Sniper rifle?" said Mel.

"Right." A single chuckle. "My father was…well…you see, the thing is that…well, I know that place."

"You do?"

"Queens Botanical Gardens? The Wedding Garden?"

"Right." He was surprised.

Once again, she looked past him into a memory. "My father called himself the 'Landscape Curator' there. That's a bit lofty. He was a gardener, a classic get-down-on-your-knees, flower-kissing dirt worshipper. That garden…when I was three, four, five years old, that was…" Her eyes misted up. This was an interesting woman. "That was my enchanted playland. I'd go to work with my dad, and he'd set me free, let me run around all day. It had everything! Flowers to sniff, bunnies to chase, golden sunlight, a gazebo, a stream. I would play hide and seek with my imaginary friends from dawn till dusk. I still dream about it." She brought her gaze back to him. "I think everyone has a personal Paradise Lost. Don't you? From when you were young?"

Mel pondered this. He was surprised by what came to mind. "Yeah. I guess for me that was the Met. Third grade teacher took me there when I was eight. I thought I was entering a royal palace of the gods." Mel was suddenly back in that moment: eight years old, staring at Monet's radiant haystacks. *A person just like me looked at the world and captured it on canvas! I wonder if I can do that?* In a moment, something awakened: a knowing of what's possible, a hunger to do something that could astonish.

Daisy asked him how he came to paint "Garden Bride, Queens." He told her the story, including the improbable rescue from his trashed half-apartment. "And now," said Mel, "it's become something we have in common."

"I guess," she said, looking down into her empty cup.

"What's the matter?"

"Paradise Lost," she said. "My dad was perfectly happy digging in the dirt all day, but my mom was outraged because he 'didn't want to make something of himself.' She had this whole Lady Macbeth scheme for him to become Chief Horticulturalist of the Central Park Conservancy, then rent himself to billionaire hedge-fund weekenders to redo their places in

Westchester, sell his own branded line of fertilizer, the whole bit. He laughed at her, so she divorced him, took everything, and forbade me ever to see him again. I was eleven. She drilled into me what a loser he was, and how we had a better chance to 'make it' without him. She went to work at a law firm, and married one of the partners, guy named Muncie Hudnutt."

"Stepfather," said Mel to say something. She nodded.

"He was interested in red wines from the Bordeaux region of France, watching the Knicks play at Madison Square Garden, and having my mother host his cocktail parties, in that order. Young Daisy Hudnutt was not on that list or any other."

"So. Your father. Ever see him again?"

"Not for years. I thought he'd forgotten me, but it was just my mom burning his letters and Christmas cards. When I was sixteen, I snuck out and found him pruning the rose bushes at the Botanical Gardens. We stayed in touch till he died eight years ago. Skin cancer. Wouldn't wear sunscreen, the bastard."

"I guess that's why you love flowers so much," said Mel. They'd outlasted the lunch crowd, and now he gazed at the rapture of blooms illuminated by the primrose haze of an early autumn afternoon in New York.

She looked at him, puzzled. "What?"

"Flowers," he said. "You know. In your limo. Here, in the bistro." She continued to stare at him. "Don't you?"

"As much as the next person, I guess. Maybe a little more, but…"

"DEEDEE!" A smiling Van Courtland DeWolfe was striding toward them, followed by granddaughter Velocity. Both were pushing bicycles. DeWolfe looked fresh from a driven grouse hunt on the Scottish moors in his tweed jacket, plaid bow tie, and wool sporting cap. His bike was a vintage Hercules 1930s British touring model with a large wicker basket affixed to the handlebars. Velocity was dressed in olive drab camo fatigues and pushed a rust-brown dumpster bike.

"Wolfey!" Daisy rose and gave him a polite peck on the cheek. "How did you know we were here, darling?"

"Didn't, dearest. Just stopped by for a spot of java on our weekly trans-borough cycling jaunt." He turned to Mel. "Heard you're going to stand your ground and do battle."

It took Mel a second to figure out what he was talking about. "Ummm, oh. Yeah. Nothing to do with the Met. I hope you're not offended…"

"Not a bit of it!" He leaned toward Mel and said in a stage whisper. "After what Holcombe Parkes did to my beloved? If you wish to challenge him to a duel, I'll happily serve as your second."

"How's the journal coming?" asked Velocity.

All eyes turned to Mel. Time to come clean. He pulled out the journal and held it up for Daisy. "Monsieur Monet left more than his artwork. He left a journal of his New York adventure. I'm translating it."

Her eyes widened. "Really?" She looked at DeWolfe. "Provenance?"

"Not definitive," he said, "but close. Certainly helps."

She turned to Mel. "Does Holcombe know?" Mel shook his head. She grinned.

"Oh my," said DeWolfe, smiling.

"I'm almost done," said Mel. "Explains everything. The artwork, why New York, why these paintings. There's even a love angle."

"Ready to share?" said Velocity.

"Tomorrow night," said Mel. "You're all invited, although I'm not sure where we should…"

"Gotcha covered," said Velocity. "The MRs have new digs."

"Not in Camden, I hope," said Mel.

Velocity waved that away. "In the Bronx. Goodbye Love Shack, hello Dream Palace. Got a place for you to crash, and a grand venue suitable for your presentation. If you want it."

"I'm in. I have to call Sam Dollar. He's invited, I presume."

"Everybody on the Claude Squad," said Velocity. "Including you, Grampa, and even your bride to be."

CHAPTER TWENTY-TWO

October 7

The next night, the Claude Squad gathered on the creaking vaudeville stage of the Dream Palace. Daisy and DeWolfe were there, along with Velocity and Demo, twenty-three Moist Robots, and the newest odd couple, Edison Ziff and Simon Brittle, Authenticators Extraordinaire. Sam Dollar was eyeballing the crowd, ready to nab any spies from Team Holcombe Parkes. He looked like a bouncer at a Marine Corps Officers Club: black body armor over a black muscle tee, black SWAT boots and a black bucket hat with the words "BADDER THAN YOU" stenciled above the brim.

Demo was fiddling with the scrap heap laptop he'd use for Mel's presentation. "Amazing what shows up at E-waste drives for prep schools," he said. Without looking up from his screen, he said, "You think Monsieur Monet woulda dug this place?"

A small blob of grey-green gloop splattered on Mel's head. He brushed it off and stared up at the khaki patch of primordial ooze encrusting the ceiling. "This is more Hieronymus Bosch's scene. Or maybe Gustav Dore."

"Yeah," said Demo.

"You think you can make this place livable?"

"Don't know," said Demo. "Probably. Fun to start over. And it beats sleeping on a bus bench."

Demo was the one who'd discovered the Dream Palace. It was, in fact, the magnificent, heartbreaking wreckage of the RKO Majestic Theatre, once the gaudiest movie palace in the Bronx and a legendary expression of Hollywood Faux French Baroque.

Mel knew this theater. When he was seven, his Aunt Edna had brought him here to see a re-release of Disney's "Cinderella." He remembered nothing of the movie, but the astonishing mural on the auditorium ceiling was seared in his memory: a brassy, crowd-pleasing C.B. DeMille enhancement of Michelangelo's Sistine Chapel ceiling, currently being swallowed by an aggressive patch of fungus. In fact, every moment of that first visit had filled him with wide-eyed wonder. He had entered an awesome lobby that mimicked the Hall of Mirrors at Versailles, with barrel-vaulted ceilings, gold drapes, and six thirty-foot lead crystal chandeliers hung from cove-lit domes. Golden cherubs guarded each corner of the coffered ceiling. A magnificent marble staircase carried him to the Grand Balcony foyer, where he stared up at an opulent, three-tiered bronze and crystal fountain.

The place had been shuttered since 1977 and was now a combination mold incubator and bat sanctuary. The roof leaked, so the carpets moldered, so the walls mildewed. Scary Jack-and the-Beanstalk vines were growing in the bathrooms. The MRs had already filled two (pilfered) dumpsters with detritus. One held a half-ton of carpeting, wallpaper, and furniture claimed by the Fungi Kingdom. The other dumpster was topped out with Hefty Contractor Bags full of beer cans, vodka bottles, crack vials, syringes, and used condoms. The place had an eerie post-apocalyptic aura. As Mel bedded down that first night on a futon in what had been the men's smoking lounge, he felt like Morlocks might drop from the ceiling and club him to death with human thighbones.

Just before he drifted off, a glint of light sparked off a broken picture frame. Mel got up to investigate. After he flicked off the glass shards, he found himself holding the water-damaged program from the Majestic's opening night: March 11, 1927. The program featured six acts of vaudeville, the Clicquot Club Eskimos directed by Harry Reser, and the premiere of "The Loves of Sunya" starring Gloria Swanson and John

Boles. Mel marveled at the Lost World of Theatrical Exhibition as he read the promotional copy on the back page:

"The Majestic Theatre is a fairy palace whose presiding genius entertains you royally with all the epic allurements that art, science, and music can proffer. It affords the same pleasures, delights, and multifarious relaxations that the Fifth Avenue mansion of Cornelius Vanderbilt afforded the Commodore. It provides succor to those desperate for a surcease from the travails of the work-a-day world. This is a Utopian Rhapsody of never-to-be-equaled beauty, both ethereal and practical. No potentate ever reveled in such luxury, such a varied array of magical amusements rendered with such solicitude, such complete fulfillment of the promise of joy. Mr. and Mrs. Moviegoer become magnificent monarchs once inside the Majestic."

"Okay, good to go," said Demo. He'd scanned Monet's artwork into his computer and used BuzzSlide, a freeware PowerPoint knockoff to build a presentation to support Mel's narrative. The Majestic movie screen was decades gone as were the theater's seven ceremonial curtains. Monet's artwork would fill a giant white luminous rectangle the MRs had painted on the theater's back wall. Mel asked his guests to sit down in their ramshackle, mismatched, AA church basement seats.

"Welcome, friends. We've gathered…"

"Just a minute," said Demo. "Surprise for you." He produced his homemade remote-control unit with the buttons, dials, sliders, and toggle switches and threw the strap over his neck. He smiled at the assembled guests. "Who's up for a trip back to 1927?" He punched the panel's largest black button and then pushed up the three most prominent sliders. The rotting corpse of the Majestic vanished. Suddenly, Mel and his cohorts were magnificent monarchs inside an astonishing gilded motion picture palace created just for them by Louis XIV. The Sistine Chapel ceiling glowed anew with three-dimensional verve. Burgundy and gold brocade tapestries hung between marble columns. Trumpet wielding cherubs heralded the entertainment to come. Demo had even programmed the music: "At Sundown," by the Clicquot Club Eskimos.

Mel gaped in wonder, then turned to Demo. "Claude would be so happy." The others rose in a standing ovation. Demo took a small bow, rolled off the music, and put the control unit on the floor next to him.

Show time. Everyone sat as he pulled out Monet's journal and lofted it in his right hand. "As you know, our good friend Claude Oscar Monet left us a journal with the trove of artwork he hid in the penthouse wall of the late, lamented Love Shack. This journal is his story of what happened, and how this artwork came to be." Mel's left hand then produced the large-format Moleskine journal he'd used for his translation. "I haven't improved his words or interpreted them or embellished them. I've turned them into English as best I could. I'm here to let Monsieur Monet tell his own story in his own words."

Mel nodded and Demo filled the white rectangle with one of Monet's self-portraits. Demo then keyed the slideshow soundtrack: Django Reinhardt and Stephane Grappelli, Quintette du Hot Club de France circa 1934. Mel then read that first entry from the day he discovered the journal. *"What follows is my account of a most extraordinary happenstance that filled the months of March to October, 1921. This journal is a message in a bottle cast upon stormy seas to be read, if ever found, as an affirmation of my artistic probity. My story is, at the same time, a tale of catastrophic miscalculation and transcendent good fortune – of calamity and benediction. It is, as night falls, an asseveration that love is a black swan, an absurd circumstance that rescues the lost and justifies the hellish struggle of the artist."*

Demo dissolved from the Monet self-portrait to a black and white photo of Georges Clemenceau from the early 1920s. *"March 9, 1921. My first visitor on this momentous day was my esteemed compatriot Georges Clemenceau. Clemenceau! Doctor! Pamphleteer! Fighter of duels, foe of traitors, champion of the avant-garde! Sponsor, ally, soul mate, brother-in-arms, inspiration, confidante! And first and foremost...my great friend."*

Mel was warming to his task. As he'd translated the journals, he'd come to experience a deeper and deeper kinship with Monet. Now he felt the great man's spirit speaking through him. *"Clemenceau! Who as President of France wrested full funding for the creation of my crowning achievement as an artist, 'Au Coeur de la Vie du France.' 'The Heart of Life in France,' a showplace for my life's work."*

Demo clicked up a Monet charcoal sketch of a magnificent temple of art, with the name emblazoned in color over the entry portal. Mel then narrated a series of Monet's sketches for galleries showcasing visual themes from his life's work: haystacks, cathedrals, poplars, train stations, the Giverny garden, etc. *"More than a museum,"* said Monet through Mel, *"this would be a living expression of my love for France. Visitors here would feel this love, and something more. They would feel they were themselves French and blessed to be so. And this inferno of benevolent Francophilia would become an eternal flame, illuminating the French spirit for a thousand years."*

Demo then flashed a cascade of Monet's dolorous weeping willows painted during the most desperate months of the Great-War-That-Failed-to-End-All-Wars. Mel narrated this cavalcade of gloom. *"Clemenceau's news could not have been worse. Catastrophic. Not two months after he'd left office, the scoundrels in the French Parliament had abrogated their agreement to fund 'Au Coeur de la Vie du France.' Georges tried to comfort me, swore to continue the fight, but we both knew it was a lost cause. Hopeless! I was cast into a bottomless pit of despair. The prospect of a proper permanent exhibition of my work had been my raison d'être, a shield against the demons that plague me: this blasted arthritis, this emphysema, the cataracts that cloud my vision. The moment he left, I cried out to the heavens."*

CHAPTER TWENTY-THREE

Mel was no longer just reading Monet's words. He WAS Monet, seized by rage. He bellowed at the moss-covered ceiling. *"Mythic god-demon! Creator-destroyer of all things! Your power to create is infinite, mine is paltry. Your color palette is boundless, mine is meager. It is your music; I have merely aspired to sing a single melody for a single moment in a way that celebrates your infinite wonder! And now you deny me this tiny satisfaction? You ignite a fire in my soul and then deny me the means to use that fire to serve you? Fine! I quit! You have defeated me! Strike me dead! I am sick and tired of being the Inadequate, tasked by the Unfathomable, to do the Impossible for the Ungrateful!"* Mel fell to his knees, shut his eyes, and opened his arms to the heavens. *"Complete your cruel demolition, fiend! Strike me dead! OBLITERATE ME!"*

A pause, and then Velocity burst into applause, leading the group in a spontaneous ovation. "Bravo!" shouted Daisy, and more cheers and huzzahs followed. Mel stood, took an abashed bow, and nodded to Demo to click the next slide. The screen flashed a Monet sketch of a handsome woman in her early 30s, dressed in funereal black. Mel looked at the sketch, and then at Daisy. He saw her eyes widen. Uncanny resemblance. Same perfect oval face, same cheekbones, same bright eyes, even the same sassy hairstyle. She looked a question at him. He nodded as Monet's description of his visitor flashed in his mind: *"A Renoir portrait as written by Balzac, but with the droll irony of Voltaire."* He took a deep breath and continued.

"This day produced a second guest: one who had witnessed my mortifying divine supplication. Her name was Euphonia Cavendish-Dupree, and she had come to Giverny from America to offer me a commission. At first, I presumed she was a doltish acolyte, come here to bask in the reflected radiance of Monet's fading glory. Part of a world tour for the nouveau riche. The Eiffel Tower at 11, scones and espresso at 12, Monet at 2, a tea dance at 4. But no."

Mel nodded at Demo, who clicked through a series of Monet sketches that revealed Euphonia's face from several angles, in a range of emotions from pensive to merry. She could have been Daisy's older sister. *"Euphonia had come here on a mission of redemption, to find absolution for a great crime she didn't commit."*

Demo threw up a photo of a hatchet-faced robber baron from the late 19th century. *"Her father was Doyle Hardwick Cavendish, the infamous Copper King of Colorado. He was a heinous villain from a Zola novel, a heartless, money-mad plutocrat who employed every means — even the murder of workers who dared to demand a living wage — to build a citadel of pelf. He perished from a stroke when he was told that Euphonia's teenage mother had died bringing her into the world. Euphonia then became the wealthiest newborn in America. As she matured, this lonely girl grew to despise the trivial social hurly-burly of moneyed society, especially her vulnerability as prey for decadent wastrels and fortune-hunting predators. She became President of the Bronx Women's Art League, and as such had been bewitched by a traveling exhibit displaying my painting 'Women in The Garden.' It inspired her to a decision: to spend her fortune to counter her father's perfidy by bringing something good and beautiful into the world. She was here to take the next step: to enlist me in her redemptive enterprise."*

Mel looked at the group. He had them: or rather, *Monet* had them. The Master's words and pictures had them rapt. He nodded at Demo, who toggled through a set of historic photos downloaded from Google Images. *"Miss Cavendish-Dupree would have me believe she was the fiancée of Monsieur Jacob Ruppert, a brewing tycoon with money troubles, as Prohibition had destroyed his lucrative beer business. Her protestations of virtue only made the truth more obvious. Euphonia was this man Ruppert's courtesan. The poor girl was dancing with the phantom of her deceased father, at once repelled by his greed and beguiled by his power. Monsieur Ruppert owned a team of sportsmen, called 'Yankees.' Euphonia had lent him the funds to purchase a master athlete for this team, named George-Babe Ruth, and now Ruppert wished to erect a monumental hippodrome – a 'park of balls,' in his words – to showcase the athletic prowess of Monsieur Ruth and his fellow Yankees for their patrons. Once again, he approached Euphonia on bended knee to loan him money. This time, she placed a condition on her munificence. She demanded that Ruppert invite Monsieur Claude Monet to become Artistic Design Director Emeritus for this Stadium of Yankee Ballers. Ruppert grudgingly agreed, hence Euphonia's lovely presence here at Giverny."*

Mel looked up at a sea of wide eyes and open mouths. Even those who suspected this story might take an unexpected turn weren't ready for this. Mel remembered his own reaction as he read, re-read, and re-re-read this passage in Monet's diary. It was wildly unexpected and completely logical: the only reasonable solution to the riddle of the artwork.

Mel then described Monet's negotiation with Euphonia. She offered him 100,000 francs. He demanded 500,000. She told him that the initial plans were complete; she just wanted Monet to... what? Mel looked into his Moleskine and read Monet's words. *"She told me the current renderings were prose, desperate for Monet's poetry."*

"They must have made some kind of deal," said Velocity. "Right? I mean, hence the artwork." The group murmured assent.

"Sure," said Mel, off-book. "But Euphonia was spending her own money, and she wouldn't budge on her offer. Monet told her...let's see." He dived back into the Moleskine, picking up Monet's voice. *"I was outraged at her effrontery. I howled, 'You want Monet? You will pay for Monet. And you will get Monet — unfettered, unbound, unconstrained! I may look like an old goat, but artistically, I'm a young stallion! I must run free! Burn these plans, we will start afresh! 500,000 francs, my final offer.'*

"To my surprise and dismay, Miss Cavendish-Dupree shrieked 'Noooooo!' and began to weep. 'It was a fool's errand,' she wailed. 'Ruppert was right, I'm such a ninny.' What I thought was a ploy was in fact the greatest amount she

could offer. Naturally, I was unsettled. My soul was aflame with this opportunity to summon my final masterpiece, my shrine, the apotheosis of everything I've learned and felt and created. Now it was slipping away. And then the same callous deity who wrested that first dream from my clenched fists visited me with a glister of inspiration: an epiphany, really.

"I turned to Euphonia. 'You have come here to offer me a job of work that will become a shrine to my labors, yes? What if,' I said, 'I bestow my designs on you in perpetuity for the price of one American dollar? You can then license their use to Colonel Ruppert for as long as needed for the triumphant realization of his massive erection. Upon the Day of Opening, the work will be returned to you, with my blessing.'

"I could see it in my mind's eye. First, this charming and starry-eyed beauty would realize her dream without depleting her own funds. At some future time, she could sell this work — mere illustration, work for hire — for a tidy sum to some doltish American bourgeois! And of course, the benefit to Monet was immense. This place would thrill the world of art, sending the value of my life's work spinning over the moons of Jupiter! And I would have my shrine, to thrill and inspire the world!

"I watched as Euphonia's anguish turned to surprise, and then glee. Whoops of joy, kisses on cheeks, flutes of Dom Perignon. I would have my dream space! Not merely a bejeweled box housing a sleepy retrospective of my work. I had in mind a new kind of place: one that would metamorphose the very nature of art itself! No longer something to stare at, the work here would offer art-lovers something they could step into and live inside! Three-dimensional, immersive, delighting the senses and stimulating the emotions! All my great themes and inspirations presented as living theater, with my patrons joining me inside the dream of ever-evolving creative inspiration! My only regret? It would not be in France, more's the pity. But if this first one found favor, who knows? Why not similar erections in Paris, London, Berlin, Madrid, Tokyo, Sydney, Moscow?"

"Now we know why he painted the stuff," said Edison Ziff. "How the hell did it end up inside the wall of the Love Shack?"

"I'm getting there, just hold on," said Mel. "I'm going to type up my notes so everyone can read the whole journal. The next part describes

Monet's glee at having a reason to live. And also his mad crush on Euphonia."

Mel nodded at Demo, who moved forward through a series of charcoal sketches of a young woman with a parasol standing on a hill. He put his nose back in the journal. *"If we were to collaborate – if we were to conjure something out of thin air made of music and fire and laughter that would last for a thousand years and cause art lovers the world over to swoon with joy – then I knew I had to capture her heart, soul, and spirit on canvas. I ordered my assistant Max to strip off the dire funeral garments she favored and array this beauty in something radiant, reckless, revelatory! I needed to drink her in. Possess her. Newly frocked in white satin, she followed me to the hill of a nearby meadow."*

Monet's charcoal sketches of Euphonia got more and more elaborate, but no painting appeared. Mel turned the page and read on. *"As I began to paint her, sixty years fell away and I was once again an ebullient neophyte, my brush a torch to illuminate the path to my destiny. I remembered why I embraced this punishing trade. I wept with gratitude and blessed this youthful, haunted beauty."*

Edison spoke up once again. "The picture he's describing: that wasn't in the trove, was it? Do you know…"

Mel shook his head. "Not in there. Don't know if he finished it, or what happened to it. I do know that after he finished, Monet and Euphonia shared a picnic lunch." Mel thumbed forward three pages and let Monet's voice flow through him. *"As the afternoon light faded from gold to amber to the sepia of a roasted chestnut, E shared her terrible secret: that she was incapable of true love, because she would ever be suspicious that even the most benign suitor was flying under false colors, fixated on purloining her millions. That's why she'd become engaged to Colonel Ruppert, a millionaire in his own right, at least until Prohibition decimated his fortune. She felt she was doomed to a life without love. My heart leapt when I heard her words, because I, too, had a secret, and it just so happened my secret was the same secret: that I, too, was incapable of love."*

Demo switched images to Monet's famous deathbed portrait of his first wife Camille. *"I told Euphonia what I had kept locked in my heart for forty years. Camille — my first wife, my precious one —gave her life for my success. She loved me with all her heart and soul, and I loved…my work.*

"She was never the same after Michel's birth, and suddenly she was on her deathbed. And there I was beside her, wracked with grief, weeping. Or at least I should have been. No, not Monet. As I stared at Camille at the very moment of her death, I found myself gazing at those tragic features and trying to identify the sequence, the gradations of color that death had imposed on her motionless face. I trembled at the shock of the colors: a revelation!

"Instead of grieving, my only thought was to sear that face in my imagination so that the moment Camille was gone, I could hasten to my studio and capture it for eternity. Which, to my everlasting shame, I did. I shared with Euphonia the very worst thing that anyone could ever know about Monet: that he was…even to himself… a kind of monster."

Demo now projected a fully realized charcoal portrait of Euphonia. In this one, unlike the others, she gazed at the viewer with a visceral intensity. Mel saw several people glance from the portrait to Daisy, and back. Mel read Monet's words. *"Was it only this morning that I was begging God to strike me dead? And then He sent not a homicidal thunderbolt but a goddess of redemption.*

"She told me that I was wrong to think of myself as a monster. She told me that I must be capable of love because my painting, "Women in the Garden," was filled with it. It had jumped off the canvas and taken her in its arms, seduced her, whispered sweet nothings in her ear, and cajoled her to 'let go,' forget the past, live in this moment and celebrate the most elemental of God's gifts — sunlight, wildflowers, the gold of a sunset on the Seine, the simple, radiant glory of a summer wheat stack. She had fallen in love with my painting, and with me. And in this moment, I fell madly in love with her.

"Love! At 81! A magnificent, impossible, transcendent catastrophe. In an instant I had a new muse, a new mission, and a new reason to battle the demons that plagued me. I will create, and with that creative act I will touch the eternal. Euphonia and I are of one mind: that the very best place to do this job of work is New York City, where the wonderment will be built. My labors will transpire in secret, to heighten the drama when the work is revealed.

"The S.S. Paris is leaving Le Havre in three days on her maiden voyage. The Park of Balls that will be the Secular Cathedral of Claude Monet will be imagined, designed, and approved for production in three months. Max will join us, of course. I will book tickets in the morning."

CHAPTER TWENTY-FOUR

Demo put up a slide that read "Monet In New York – Sketchbook." Mel looked up from the Moleskine. "So, the great man arrives in New York and takes up residence – guess where – in the penthouse of the Ziegler-Haversham Building, with a view of the building site."

"Of course," said Demolition. "Duh…"

Mel smiled. "Here Monet more or less abandons his narrative. This part of his journal is sketches and impressions of New York in 1921. His words don't necessarily correlate to what he's sketching."

Demo put up the first image: a pencil sketch of the Brooklyn Bridge at dawn, with the Woolworth Building looming in the background.

Mel read Monet's words. *"New York is an astonishment. It's as if I've awakened inside Coleridge's opium dream of a modern-day Xanadu. It is the most astounding man-made counterfeit of the natural world: fathomless sunless canyons spewing rivers of asphalt through staggering summits of concrete and steel. This dream world is intricate and variegated, a richly figured crazy quilt, a geometry overgrown with complex designs, all lit by a million fabricated fluorescent suns."*

The next image: the Giant Racer rollercoaster of Coney Island on a frantic Saturday afternoon.

"I've never felt so alone and blessed to be so – apart yet animated by the infectious joy of the crowd's shrieking laughter. I am the one celebrating the many, unfettered and exhilarated by a dizzy overwhelm of new sensations."

Next sketch: Times Square at night, a riot of light and movement.

"The entire city is a great collision: 19th and 20th centuries, the prosperous and the penniless, light and dark, squalor and grandeur, sin and salvation, the ravishing and the repulsive, heaven and hell. Imagine a Beethoven symphony squeezed into ten seconds with every note played by an orchestra of anvils being pounded by sledgehammers."

Next: Dawn, Ebbets Field, exterior.

"Even the sporting venues are magnificent, gaudy secular cathedrals — prodigious palaces for the worship of sun-burnished athletic gods."

Finally, several sketches of the New York skyline from different angles.

"Insolent. Audacious. Brazen. New York has the irreverence of a bumptious adolescent savant. And big! Big buildings, big money, big noise, big smells, big crowds, big dreams! Never before such a terrible wonder: a mechanical phoenix powered by a perpetual motion mechanism that manufactures sensation, pleasure, and amplitude for a teeming mass of humanity. Every language is spoken, every appetite is sated, every purse is emptied.

"London is for empire, Paris for romance, New York for ambition. As I plunge into my task, I needn't worry about finding the vitality to do the work. A simple window suffices. Once opened, it provides a bracing shock of the same etheric energy that enables the perpetual motion of planets, stars, and universes.

"My job is to embrace this dream and create a dream yet greater, something that will re-introduce the biotic forms of nature into this histrionic spectacle of mechanical mass enchantment. This place will be the apotheosis of my life's work.

"So happy now. I've finally been given a canvas big enough to create what I came here to accomplish. In the moment of creation, I am eternal."

Once again Mel put down the Moleskine. "Now you're going to see the paintings, only this time illumined by Monsieur Monet's own words. This is the key entry in the diary. He is literally crafting his presentation to Yankees owner Jacob Ruppert, the one he'll deliver in Ruppert's office the next day. This is his second-to-last entry." Mel nodded to Demo, who put up a vintage black and white photograph of the exterior of Yankee Stadium, circa opening day 1923.

Mel read from the Moleskine. *"Monsieur Ruppert, first let me extend my humblest apologies. I have exceeded the boundaries of my original task. Euphonia is blameless – she has not seen the work I've completed over the last three months. I only hope you will embrace the ambition of my dream and – if I may be so bold – the genius of my accomplishment. You see, I was stunned to discover that your magnificent erection, as originally conceived, would only host devotees of baseball 77 days of the year. What I propose…"*

Mel glanced at Demo, who replaced the photo with Monet's painting of the Yankee Stadium exterior rendered as one of his famous "cathedral series" from the 1880s: "Rouen Cathedral, Full Sunlight — Harmony in Blue and Gold." The familiar Yankee Stadium name was replaced by something else, in French.

"'Au Coeur de la Vie du America' — the Heart of Life in America. A vital, living work of art for the people of the world that they can enjoy 365 days a year. Notice, Monsieur Ruppert, that the thing itself is a work of art, rendered in subtle shades of cobalt blue, cadmium yellow, vermillion, and viridian, ever-changing as the quality of daylight changes! What artist will be able to resist coming here to capture it on canvas! And to ensure they come, two unique expressions of Monet's genius…"

Demo put up the sketch of steam vaporizers ringing the top of the stadium facade.

"First, twenty-seven hundred electric water vaporizers ringing the top of the facade. You will never be dependent on the weather to produce a lambent glow for the premises, oh no! Turn on the vaporizers — Voila! The entire monument enshrouded in fog, softening the colors, and diffusing the light! Catnip for artists!"

Now Demo put up an elaborate mechanical drawing of the stadium perched atop a colossal turntable with an incredibly complex, impossibly huge wheel, gear, and pulley mechanism to turn it, driven by triple-expansion steam engines like those that powered the Titanic.

Mel continued. *"Who but Monet could conceive of something so audacious yet practical? We will build 'Au Coeur de la Vie du America' — the entire edifice — on top of the largest turntable ever constructed! It's all about the LIGHT, Colonel Ruppert! This turning mechanism will rotate the* stadium to travel with the sun throughout the day, ensuring that artists who come here from around the world will always discover the thing in its richest chromatic glory! This is just the outermost manifestation of Monet's genius. Now let's venture inside this enchanted wonderwork."

Demo projected the painting of the stadium outfield, with a Yankees player next to one of Monet's famous wheat stacks.

"You've provided me with a meadow. To complete this meadow — wheat stacks, reflecting the subtlest shades of spring, autumn, and winter light! Your patrons will weep with gratitude at the chance to paint them. And the outfield fence! Begging for Monet magic!"

Demo switched to the painting of the outfield fence improved by Monet.

"'Les Nympheas,'" said Mel as Monet. "The fence becomes a mural for an astonishing expanse of Monet water lilies, with the warning track a reflecting pond! Magnificent! Let us now move to the infield."

Demo clicked the painting that showed the famous Giverny Japanese Bridge now spanning a koi pond infield. First base, third base, and the pitcher's mound were tiny islands.

"See? The infield is now a signature sunken garden filled with koi, water lilies, and aquatic flora. It's spanned by a Japanese bridge, covered with purple and white wisteria. Notice how it unifies first and third base! The pitcher's mound is an island that is easily reachable by rowboat. Imagine the thrill of your spectators seeing clouds and sky perfectly reflected in the crystalline waters! And now the viewing stands…"

Demo put up the painting of the grandstands as a massive flower garden, no seats to be seen.

Mel read Monet's words with the kind of brash enthusiasm Mel imagined Monet brought to the actual pitch. "Instead of fixed seats, each patron will bring his or her own folding chair and seat him or herself in the midst of a glorious garden — a riot of roses, hollyhocks, dahlias, nasturtiums, begonias. Your attendance will triple! Sporting enthusiasts can watch the sporting activity. Artists can paint the field! Gardeners can breathe in the fragrance and bask in the color of the extant flora! Something for everyone! And to complement this feast for the senses, a feast for the stomach."

Demo showed a colored sketch of an elaborate French open-air brasserie festooned with Yankees pennants.

"This is a place of joy — of celebration. I propose that you offer comestibles worthy of the astonishment I've revealed. Pâté en croûte, wild rabbit and duck terrines, well-hung oven-roasted woodcock, foie gras — from the Alsace region only — and pigeon stew, from my personal recipe. For dessert, blueberry-mascarpone roulade and gâteau basque."

Demo returned to the slide of Yankee Stadium as the Rouen Cathedral. *"I have given you my best, Monsieur Ruppert. Instead of 77 days a year, our wonderment will inspire your patrons 365 days a year. Instead of just New York sporting enthusiasts, it will draw millions of art lovers from around the world. It will redefine the nature of the art museum, from a dank, passive catacomb to a sun-washed, open-air living experience that invites everyone to pick up a brush and find the Monet in themselves! I stand ready to supervise the construction of the facility and the installation of my work. Even better – and this is my final gift to you and the glorious woman we both love, the goddess who has given me this opportunity, our beloved Euphonia – I make you a solemn promise. On Opening Day, I will become your Artist in Residence. I will remain here in New York for one year to greet our new patrons. I will join them as they capture the magic of this place.*

"Together, we will generate a robust body of work that will astonish the world and supersede whatever revenues are generated by mere seasonal sporting endeavors."

Mel let the room settle for a moment before the last diary entry. Previous entries had revealed why Monet did the paintings. As he'd read Monet's words with the symphony of images, he was struck by something in the room: or rather, the lack of something. Coughing. Squirming. Twitching. The crinkle of candy wrappers. The magnificent, absurd, doomed ambition of the great man was even more compelling than it must have been back in 1921. "I wish I could end this presentation right here," said Mel. "I wish this story had a different, better ending. But it doesn't."

CHAPTER TWENTY-FIVE

Mel turned the page of the Moleskine. His voice was now a husky rasp, both from exhaustion and emotion. He was taking this journey with them, and this was the final stop.

"The meeting with Yankees owner Jacob Ruppert took place on October 14, 1921," said Mel, setting up the last entry. "Ruppert could not have been in a good humor, since the Yankees had lost the World Series to their hated cross-town rivals, the Giants, the day before, and Ruppert's expensive acquisition, Babe Ruth, had failed to distinguish himself. I...uhhh, that is, Monsieur Monet has no journal entry for this meeting. The final journal entry is October 17, 1921. This entry is a draft of a letter to Euphonia." He started to say more, but he could read the crowd – shut up and get to it. Demo put up two images, side by side: the color self-portrait of Monet and Monet's final, definitive charcoal portrait of Euphonia. Mel picked up the Moleskine and read.

"My dearest Euphonia: please don't think I am filled with despair because of the debacle with your fiancé. Yes, he defamed me and threw me bodily from his office. Yes, I presumed – falsely – that you'd join me in exile. I was thunderstruck when you, for whatever reason, refused my entreaty to join me in Giverny and chose instead to stay in America with this insensitive boor. I've done nothing but ponder this since we parted and, in so doing, anguish has become equanimity. You may be surprised to discover that I am sanguine. Happy, even. And blessedly content.

"Why? Because of you, dearest one. Before we met, I thought of myself as a monster, incapable of love. I was facing my death thinking that my life had been in vain, that I had failed at my only important task — to know love, to bring it to my work, and to share it with the world. You, dearest one, you opened your heart and revealed to me the meaning of my own life, a meaning that I'd hidden from myself."

Mel lowered the Moleskine, took a deep breath, and looked at Daisy. Her eyes were wide. Mel felt his heart race. Monet's words were his words. He brought the notebook up and continued.

"What you felt when you saw my paintings is what I felt when I painted them. Love! Because of you I know I have not worked in vain. All those years, all that labor, pain, and suffering. It was all worth it if it made you happy for a single moment.

"I spent my life thinking I was painting to satisfy some judgmental, cranky muse, but no! I was painting for you, so that our two hearts could share joy across decades, continents! And that joy led to our work together, this greatest of follies that has produced moment after moment of inspired, loving creative pleasure.

"It makes no difference what you and Colonel Ruppert do or don't do, because the work lived, in that room, for one wonderful moment! And the great love that inspired the work — that still lives, more alive than ever. Precious, priceless, ethereal, transcendent. The two of us sharing our love in a single, eternal moment."

Mel paused again, moving the notebook up to cover his face. Tears pricked his eyes. He felt the anguish of Monet's gratitude. He continued, his voice almost a whisper.

"Good-bye, my dearest one. No one will ever see the artistic wonders we conjured together, I have made certain of that. The work is ours and ours alone, now and forever. I hope you find happiness with Monsieur Ruppert. You've given this old man a magnificent gift of unexpected, unearned, unforeseen happiness. My gift to you is but a paltry bagatelle in return. Sealed with a love that will last forever, Claude."

Mel brought the Moleskine down and looked again at Daisy. Her hand veiled her bowed head, hiding her tears. The silence was finally broken by Velocity. "He said 'the gift.' What was the gift?"

"Not sure," said Mel. "Might be the missing Monet: the portrait of Euphonia he started that day in that meadow."

"Makes sense. Hell of a wedding present," said Ziff.

"Yeah," said Sam Dollar, "But Jacob Ruppert never got married." He held up his smartphone. "So says the almighty Wikipedia. And yes, I crosschecked with other sources. 'Lifelong confirmed bachelor who left the Yankees to his brother and sister.'"

"The Moist Robots have an announcement," said Velocity. "You are invited – with the understanding that you have no choice – to continue pondering this mystery at a reception and buffet in our Carole Lombard Grand Salon. If you hate the food, complain to our resident wizard of organic, locavore, GMO and cruelty-free cuisine, Bartholomew "Bean Sprout" Metcalfe."

CHAPTER TWENTY-SIX

When Demo's trusty crowbar had busted open the rusted-out steel door to the forgotten, walled-off theater sub-basement chamber marked "MANAGERIAL STORAGE – NO ADMITTANCE," he and his cohorts discovered a secret. One Ajax McKeewie, manager of the RKO Majestic from 1932 to 1946, had apparently been conducting a mad, passionate love affair with screwball film goddess Carole Lombard without her knowing a single thing about it.

Amidst rotting boxes of Salem Tricorne China plates from a failed "Dish Night" promotion and cardboard shout-outs for the "Baby Parade This Saturday!", the MRs found a twenty-drawer cherry wood flat file cabinet filled with posters for every feature film Ms. Lombard made from 1932 to her death in 1942. These magnificent posters now decorated the bile-green concrete walls of what had been the theater's Mechanical Refrigeration Room.

Mel was agog at the vivid, captivating paper-on-canvas posters. Lombard's allure was as bewitching as ever, undimmed after eighty years. There she was, tragic in "No More Orchids," madcap in "My Man Godfrey," and otherworldly in "Supernatural." His favorite was Lombard with a magnificent shiner in "Love Before Breakfast." Twenty-three posters in all, most better than the movies they promoted.

The MRs spread was a quirky deep-dive into PETA-approved veganistical cuisine: millennial chic buttressed by fearless scavenging from au courant restaurant dumpsters. Sam Dollar eyeballed the spread with disdain. "There's a reason we kill and eat cows, you know. It's so they don't multiply and take over the planet."

"My favorite kind of customer!" said Metcalfe, a jolly, bearded foodie in a homemade 'Peace, Love and Veggie Burgers' apron. "Here, I made something just for you," He handed Sam a blue enamel camp-style dinner plate and heaped it with food. "Mushroom lentil bourguignon inside a volcano of roasted garlic smashed potatoes. Never met a meathead who didn't go wild over this."

"You didn't sneak any tofu into it, did you?" Metcalfe smiled and shook his head as he handed a plate to Mel, next in line. He filled his plate with barley risotto, roasted cauliflower, and arugula salad as Mel looked for Wolfey. Where was he?

Mel topped his Flintstones jelly jar (Wilma) with jug red wine and waded into the crowd. He saw Daisy standing with Demo and Velocity. He watched her throw her head back and hoot with glee as she stood beneath the ethereal Lombard laughing at Jack Benny on the poster of "To Be or Not To Be." *Of course, that's it. So obvious.* Daisy was magnificent in the same way Lombard was. Smart, fast, funny, and so damn beautiful, but not the least bit stuck up about it. Heaven and earth in one woman.

All his life he'd dreamed of meeting a beautiful, smart woman who could laugh at herself and at life, who *was in on the joke.* Now here she was, and she was orbiting a different planet, engaged to Daddy Warbucks. He walked up to her and said as off-handedly as he could, "Where's Wolfey?"

"Oh, he had another fundraiser. Central Park Conservancy. They want to re-do the Carousel."

Velocity cut in front of him. "Monet's story was kickass!" she said, flicking a fingertip of edamame hummus into her mouth. "Those sketches of Euphonia, wow! Monet was seriously crushin' on her."

"Yeah," said Demo. "And did you guys notice how much she looked like Daisy? I mean, wow, it was like her older sister!"

A short, awkward pause. Daisy looked at the floor. "Ummm, no," said Mel, lying. "I, ummm, didn't…that is, now that I think of it…well…Daisy? Did you notice…"

Daisy turned to Velocity. "Bartholomew's a genius. I'm having some more of those scrumptious quinoa-kale patties," and walked back to the buffet table. All three watched her leave.

"Did I say something wrong?" said Demo.

"She acts like she's freaked out," said Velocity.

"About what?" said Demo. He and Velocity turned to Mel.

"Not a clue," he lied again.

．　．　．

Half an hour later, Mel was stuffed and mellow from a second jelly jar of vin ordinaire. Velocity called the after-meeting to order. As she jumped up on the just-cleared buffet table in her paint-spattered camo pants, 'Dumpster Diving Diva' t-shirt and Doc Martens, Mel thought of Demo's description of her as a 'G.I. Jane Guerilla Art Commando Action Figure.' "So, let's figure out where we are and what we're up against." She turned her head. "Daisy?"

"Where we are is that we're pretty sure Claude Monet painted this stuff, correct?" Every head bobbed at Daisy.

"Not that we can prove it," said Edison Ziff, refilling his jelly jar (Pebbles) for the fifth time. Mel admired real Bohemians who could drink all night without getting tipsy.

"But Monet's journal could be a huge help in court," said Daisy. "Which leads to me to what we're up against. In exactly one week, October 14th at 9 a.m., the Surrogate's Court of the City of New York will hold a hearing in front of the right honorable Judge Lafcadio Banks to decide if there's any reason this artwork should not be placed in the stewardship of the New York Metropolitan Museum of Art."

"One week?" said Simon Brittle. "What's the rush?"

"Seems my ex-husband has created an ad hoc 'visionary alliance' with the Met, the Mayor, and our City Council rep to fast-track his casino-condo project. They're already gold-plating the shovels for the ground-breaking."

"Hold on. Why does the Met get it? Mel found it," said Velocity, peeved.

"WE found," said Mel. "It belongs to all of us."

"Or maybe none of us," said Daisy.

Mel froze mid-sip. He put his jar down and felt the wine burn a hole in his stomach. "None of us? You mean…"

"I've looked at this thing every which-way," said Daisy. "And, well…"

"Give it to us straight," said Sam.

"The diary establishes a clear line of ownership to Euphonia Cavendish-Dupree. If she has any heirs…"

"No heirs that we know of," said Sam Dollar. "The trail goes stone cold in 1921."

"Okay then." Daisy now assumed the neutral tone lawyers reserved for death row inmates whose last appeal has just been denied. "The New York City Housing Authority seized the Love Shack in 1988 after the slumlords who owned it walked away. They put it up for auction seven times, with no takers. The Housing Authority therefore owned it when Mel found the art, and so…well…every bit of the law that I can find defaults to ownership by the city of New York."

"NO!" shouted Velocity. "We've got 'em, and we're gonna keep 'em."

"The possession argument is null here," said Daisy. "The law says that whoever is in actual custodial possession of property is presumed to be the rightful owner in the absence of clear and compelling documentation of a direct heir. Virtually every precedent supports this."

"No wiggle room at all?" said Mel.

"There's always wiggle room," said Daisy. "And we're going into court to wiggle our asses off."

"Yeah!" said Velocity.

"What's our case?" said Mel.

Daisy smiled and looked at Simon. "A certain legendary art historian friend of ours will offer his expertise."

"The city was a neglectful steward of this work, to say the least," said Simon. "Disgraceful. Melvin rescued it. Saved these cultural treasures from crumbling into dust. Man's a hero, and the paintings should be his reward."

"That's worth a try," said Daisy. "And I'm researching some cases where the courts used, let us say, 'vast discretion' in awarding long-lost art to private parties. It's not much, but it gives us a ten to twenty percent chance. If barrister Banks is sympatico, who knows what might happen?"

"Worth a try," said Mel. Nobody spoke for several seconds. *We're dead* thought Mel. *Dang. Got this far, and now…*

"I wonder if I could bend your collective ear for a sec," said Simon. He stared at the floor, gathering his thoughts. "Something about this whole megillah that bothers the hell outta me."

"What's that?" asked Mel.

"Euphonia." He paused as if his concern should be obvious to the group.

"What about her?" said Velocity.

"She was all set to tie the knot with Jake Ruppert, yes? Her long-time squeeze? In a matter of days? Big society wingding? And then suddenly, nothing. What happened?"

"Good question," said Sam Dollar.

"What went down after the debacle in Ruppert's office?" said Simon. "Lovestruck heiress vanishes without a trace. Really? Did the poor gal ever get hitched again? Her millions must have gone somewhere, making some lucky bastard very happy. Where, and to whom?"

"Keep going," said Daisy.

Simon began to pace. "Did they ever see each other again? I mean, Euphonia and Monet. The old coot was over the moon about her, and she was over that very same moon."

"And what about that painting of her?" said Velocity. "The one he gave her for a wedding present? What did she do with it? There's a loose end. Why isn't it on calendars and t-shirts and stuff?"

"There's gotta be more to this story, doncha think?" said Simon. "Shouldn't we, I dunno…."

"What?" said Daisy.

Simon looked at her, and then at Mel. "Do something?"

"Like?" said Velocity.

"Like…" Simon's brow furrowed. "Giverny. Whatever we're looking for is probably there." He looked at Mel. "Let's send Melvin there to poke around."

Mel was dumbfounded. "Me?"

"Who else?' said Simon.

"Makes total sense," said Velocity.

"He could go while I get ready for the court hearing," said Daisy.

"But the airfare, it costs a fortune to…"

"Seven hundred seventy-one dollars round trip," said Demo, pounding away at his keyboard. "WanderYonder.com, special super saver fare, New York to Paris changing planes in Lisbon. This rate is good for one hour."

"Really?" said Mel. "I, ummm…" *This is happening too fast.*

"It's a red eye. You gotta be willing to leave at midnight," said Demo. "And serve drinks to the other passengers."

"That's chump-change," said Sam Dollar. You're goin', little buddy. And I'm payin' for it."

"I'm in for half," said Daisy.

"I'm in for half of her half," said Edison Ziff.

"I'll pitch in half of Sam's half," said Simon.

"Book it," Sam ordered Demo.

"Leave tomorrow night?" Demo was looking at Mel, his hand poised over the "Confirm" key.

"NO!" Mel shouted. Everyone stared at him. "I mean…that is, I have something to do tomorrow, all day, very important." He turned to Sam. "Are you sure you want to…."

"Shut up and take yes for answer," said Sam.

"Before we sober up," added Ziff.

"Something there, genius," said Simon. "Find it."

The party wound down with French press coffee, chocolate-filled almond butter cookies and salted caramel cupcakes. Mel was savoring a decaf coffee with a healthy splash of 'Widowmaker' Brooklyn-crafted artisanal whiskey kicked in by Sam Dollar. Quite an indulgence, but he needed a jolt of audacity for the work he had to do.

Daisy drifted over to him holding her own glass of the whiskey. "Sorry the news was so grim," said Daisy. "You probably turned down a perfectly good job at the Met for nothing."

The coffee drink was working. Mel felt a cozy glow warm his body from his hair follicles to the soles of his feet. "Nah. Me? I couldn't be happier."

She was taken aback. "You are? You're probably going to lose everything."

"Not everything," said Mel. "I've got some new friends. I've got an amazing trove of artwork, at least temporarily. And my friend Claude has inspired me pick up the brush. For the first time in twenty years I'm painting again."

"How wonderful!" said Daisy. "Have you told Simon? He'll be thrilled. What are you working on?"

"Nothing yet. I start tomorrow morning."

"Know what you're going to paint?"

The smidge of caffeine in the decaf sparked up the whiskey just enough to push Mel's gumption button. "Yes. You."

Daisy went wide-eyed, then shook her head, stunned. "M-me?"

"Yes."

"You want to paint *me*?"

Mel knew he had to get her to say yes right now, and the date had to be tomorrow. If she thought about it, he was dead. "You're the one, Daisy. There's something in you that inspires me the way Euphonia inspired…that is…you are my Euphonia, Daisy. I want to…no, make that *need* to capture you on canvas."

"But…"

"With you as my muse, I can rewrite my life story. You are my breakthrough."

"Gee, I don't know…" Mel had to close the deal. He had to get her wild, dirt-worshipping father side to agree before her sensible, rifle-wielding mother side shut everything down. "I'm very busy. When exactly would you want me to…"

"Tomorrow. *That's* the important thing I've got to do before I go to France."

"Where…"

"Wedding Garden, Queens Botanical Gardens," said Mel.

She let out a small gasp. "But…can I…can you just let me, you know, think about it…"

"You and I both think about things way too much, don't we, Daisy? It's one day, that's all. Maybe I'll humiliate myself tomorrow, but who knows? Maybe, just maybe I've still got it. Simon believes in me. Do you?"

"Look, I'd love to help you, but…"

"Maybe you'll enjoy yourself. Maybe…" He hesitated.

"What?"

"Maybe I'll show you something in yourself you didn't know was there."

"But…"

"One day."

"But…"

"Just show up."

"But…"

"I'm going home now to rest up. See you tomorrow morning, 11 a.m. Wear something memorable." And then Mel race-walked away before she could say another word.

CHAPTER TWENTY-SEVEN

October 8

The voice was back, screaming at him.

You're an idiot.

Mel knew this voice well. This was the voice that had kept him artistically inert for decades.

You're a nothing. Be smart! Avoid humiliating yourself! Leave art making to the real artists!

And right now?

How could you be so stupid? You're going to disgrace yourself in front of the woman you love. Bonehead!!!

Mel had no one to blame but himself. He's the one who asked Daisy to show up at the Queens Botanical Garden at 11 a.m. wearing "something memorable." And here she was in a period-perfect white silk gown with a billowing skirt, finished with decorative emerald ribbon bows that caused his heart to vault into his throat. It was just like the dress Camille wore when she'd posed for Monet's "Woman with a Parasol." Daisy had even managed to find a matching bonnet and jade-green antique parasol with an ivory silk cover, silk fringe and tassel, and hand-carved ivory handle.

Mel was dripping with flop sweat. He'd set up his two easels, so he could do what, exactly? One easel braced his blank canvas. The other held a reference print of "Woman with a Parasol," with a mini-print of Monet's "Self-Portrait with a Beret" alligator-clipped to the bottom. The late autumn weather was just what he'd hoped for: temperature in the crisp mid-60's, billowy clouds scudding across an azure sky. Daisy was ready to give herself to him. Mel had the gear, the garden, and the girl. All he lacked was the nerve and the talent. This was going to be the face-plant of a lifetime.

Mel cast a bleak glance at his empty canvas, then at Daisy, then at Monet's gruff visage. He gasped for air. He considered throwing down his palette and speed-walking away, not stopping until he found a graveyard with a nice, deep hole he could jump into, pulling the sod in after him. An anxious tremor in his right hand sealed his fate. He was George Armstrong Custer at the Little Big Horn surrounded by homicidal Lakotas. He opened his mouth to apologize to Daisy.

"Stop thinking. PAINT!"

He froze. The voice was in his mind. It wasn't the familiar whisper of doom he knew so well. This voice was raspy, ancient, and...holy shit...French. "Who said that?" he muttered.

"Who do you think?"

Mel looked about him. There was Daisy, waiting. Just behind her, a single pony-tailed twenty-something female in overalls and hip waders was troweling in a bed of trumpet daffodils. Daisy looked at him in alarm. "Is something wrong?"

"Wrong? Ummm, no! Nothing's wrong." He was losing it. His face felt pale, clammy. His eyes were pinpricks. "Can you give me, umm, five minutes?" Annoyance flashed across her face. Then she nodded, closed her parasol, pulled a smartphone out of her bodice, and began flipping through her emails. Mel's eyes swiveled slowly to the small self-portrait of Monet. His mind broadcast the words, "Was that your voice? Are you talking to me? You are, aren't you?"

"Is there a doubt in your mind?"

"No."

"Why have you spent so many hours staring at my paintings?"

"B-because, ummm..."

"Because they speak to you. They stir something deep in your soul, like the writings in my journal, because there is something you yourself want to bring into this world. That is why I have answered your call."

"My call?"

"You've staked your life on this moment have you not? Seize it! This is all that ever was, is now, and ever shall be! Fail like I did! With a mad passion!"

"But…"

"There's the cliff. JUMP!"

"But…"

"Take a charcoal. Call her back. NOW!"

"DAISY!" She turned with a start. Mel realized he'd yelled at her. "Ummm, the sun. It's just right. I'm ready. Could you, ahhh, stand where you were before? Open parasol, facing the breeze?" She tucked her smartphone back in her bodice and took a slightly stiff, 'artistic' position, her idea of an artist's model. Mel's hand hovered over the canvas. He looked at Monet. *"Now what?"* he thought.

"She must relax."

He looked at Daisy. "Can you…ummm…you need to relax." Daisy smiled, eased her shoulders, and softened her pose. Back to Monet. *"And now?"*

"Now remember the first moment your heart burst with the thought of creating something that would cause others to feel the joy you were feeling in the moment of creation. Before you knew there were rules. Before your mind crushed your emotions."

Mel shut his eyes and found himself back in that moment. Eight years old, first trip to the Met, eyes wide, mouth agape, staring at "Haystacks, Effect of Snow and Sun." He could feel the hot tears that burned his cheeks as he drank in that epic painting, euphoric in knowing that such a thing existed, and it was here, in New York, where he lived, and he could visit it any time he wanted, and maybe, just maybe, he could figure out a way to do something like it.

"Now look at her."

"Okay." He looked at her, then turned to the canvas and brought the charcoal pencil up to the canvas.

"NO!" Mel flinched, then froze. *"Not yet. Look at her again. REALLY LOOK."* Mel looked. Daisy was glancing at him, as Camille had glanced at Monet in "Parasol."

"What am I looking for?"

"You are looking for the thing in her that's inside yourself." Monet's voice in his head was softer, barely audible. *"An emotion she stirs in you. The reason you've chosen this woman in this moment to be your inspiration."* The anxiety started to melt as Mel stared at Daisy. Finally – FINALLY – he began to see her. *"You've staked your life on this moment. Why? How does she make you feel? Why is it absolutely vital, the most important thing in the world, that you capture this woman on canvas? Here, today, now?"*

Mel smiled. "She's…she's…well, let me put it this way. My best friend blasted me with fifty thousand volts of electricity a couple of days ago. That's how I feel when I'm near her, except in a happy way."

"So, you love her."

"Yes!" Mel laughed. Mel Flack, abject failure, was in love with the gorgeous fiancée of a charismatic billionaire. And she was his for this one perfect day. He stared at her as Monet spoke.

"Paint that love. Paint the music you hear when you think of her. Paint the light inside her only you can see. Paint the divine mystery that brought you together with her. Nothing else matters. That's what drove me. Let it drive you as well. You have no past and no future, just this one defining moment. The soul demands the fullest expression of its desires. It is here for its own joy. Revel in that joy, and let it carry you along."

• • •

The surprising thing for Mel, after all the panic and suicidal thoughts and sweaty, shaking palms and mental uproar, was just how *simple* it was to sketch Daisy, and then bring that sketch alive with color. Not easy; nothing easy about it. Mel had to go back fifty years to *feel* what sparked his imagination at eight years old. Then he had to use that spark to light a fire in his soul. But once that spark was lit, it was as simple as "don't think, paint."

Monet went silent as Mel painted, but no matter. His words were the music that echoed in Mel's mind as he painted his love for Daisy, just trying to capture her inner light. He wasn't even sure who was doing all this great work. Was it Mel or Monet? Mel was holding the brush, but how was he mixing the colors of Monet's late palette so easily, by instinct? Melvin Flack was a blocked, self-doubting dead-loss as a painter, so who was this guy who was practically dancing with his canvas? Dabbing it with ease and chuckling to himself as the work got done?

One hour after his charcoal pencil had touched the canvas, he put his brush down and looked at what he'd achieved. His head snapped back in amazement. A basic sketch usually took him an hour. He had finished this one in twenty minutes. He'd spent another twenty completing an underpainting that fixed the sky, the garden, and the structural elements of Daisy's figure. Then he focused on what he loved about that enchanting face.

His exhilaration – he was *doing it*, and it was *good!* – was heightened by a wistful, bittersweet remembering. The years – decades – of paralyzing self-doubt that curdled into self-loathing. The butterfly, earthbound, berated by a cascade of snails, from his mother to his college profs to his ex-wife to Dwayne Mallard. Oh, the *freedom* to soar above them, watch them disappear, was so…so *liberating*.

Mel glanced at "Woman with a Parasol" and marveled at how his painting of Daisy rhymed with that of the master. There was the slight breeze that rustled Daisy's gown, and the streaks of green, yellow, and red that animated the grass and the garden. Mel even went the master one better by capturing Daisy's exquisite face. Monet had hidden Camille's face behind a blue veil. Mel would not be denied. The eyes were the hardest. How to capture that sparkle? Transparent blue green, an aquamarine that whispered turquoise. *Too hard…don't know how…maybe if I stopped now…* Mel caught himself. *THINKING AGAIN. STOP IT.* He took three deep breaths, then let his brush do the work. A daub of Cobalt blue, a dab of emerald green, a dot of cadmium yellow. Now paint the love. Yes. More. Good. *Exactly.*

Mel took a step back and looked at what he'd done. Not ready for a gallery wall, but...what's the word...*worthy*. Like the portrait of his Puerto Rican muse in this same Wedding Garden twenty years ago. This was the inspired work of a talented artisan.

Daisy fidgeted. She was getting bored. He put his palette down on the concrete bench and nodded to her. She came over to him, her collapsed parasol a walking stick. She paused before crossing the line to Mel's side of the canvas, to make sure he wanted her to see what he'd done. He nodded again, and then she was beside him, looking at her picture.

She stared at it, then looked at Mel, then back at the painting. She took a step back so she could compare it to Monet's "Parasol," then moved toward it once more. She grinned, squealed, and wrapped Mel in a boa constrictor hug that went on for half a minute. "You like it?" he asked, sure of the answer. She laughed, took him in her arms, and kissed him – full, lush, on the lips, a kiss to build a dream on. Then she pulled back, looked him in the eye, and pulled him into another hug. Mel closed his eyes. He was having a remember-on-your-death-bed moment, and he knew it. He drank it in.

CHAPTER TWENTY-EIGHT

The distinctive picnic blanket was courtesy Mel's pal Demolition. It was, in fact, one of Velocity's dumpster finds – an off-white, vinyl-backed drop cloth, spattered with so much paint it looked like a lesser work of Jackson Pollock. Demo had 'borrowed' it from the floor of her art studio and customized it for Mel's picnic with Daisy. The blanket now featured stylized renderings of the exact foodstuffs that Monet had painted at the bottom-center of his "Luncheon on the Grass." There was the whole roasted chicken, the terrine, the jumble of fruits, the loaf of bread and the two bottles of wine. Mel was unsurprised when Daisy laughed at the joke, quickly ticking off the painting, the food, the picnickers, and the year. "The poor man was starving to death when he painted this," she said. "He was dead broke. I'm sure he chose this subject matter so he could eat the leftovers after he dismissed his models."

They'd washed down Velocity's Tofurkey and avocado sandwiches and broccoli slaw with a modest Chenin Blanc. Now they were wafting through the afternoon on the clouds of afterglow. Mel was perched on the picnic blanket, with Daisy propped against his chest so he could inhale the floral scent of her hair.

Relaxed and happy. Mel was probably the happier of the two. He'd finally gotten the 600-pound gorilla of failure off his back, at least for one day. Not only could he paint, he'd somehow managed to summon the spirit of Claude Monet as his Guardian Angel/personal coach/soul-guide.

He didn't know how he'd done it, or if he could do it again. He'd think about that tomorrow. This was his day with Daisy. In love with Daisy. *His* Daisy, just this one lovely day. Tomorrow he'd be back in the world, and this day would be a rapturous, melancholy memory.

"Man, this is your classic Italian wedding," said Daisy, gazing toward the gazebo. Mel couldn't have planned a better entertainment. Just as he uncorked the wine for their picnic, the extended families of young Nicholas 'Nicky' Tagliagamba and Valentina 'Tina' Lombardozzi had come together to join this couple in connubial bliss. Now the postnuptial bash was in full swing.

"What makes it a classic?" asked Mel.

"Well, for starters," mused Daisy, "our Tina's about five months preggers." Mel thought she was a little pudgy, but now... yeah, right. "Second, look at all those matching apricot prom dresses. The bride has, like, twenty-three bridesmaids."

"Why so many?"

"My guess? She had to ask every one of her cousins because World War Three would have broken out if she'd chosen just the ones she liked. And finally: check out the parents sitting next to the dance floor. Notice anything peculiar?"

"No. I mean, well...the mother on the right looks like a Mafia hit woman. Veil, dark glasses, black suit..."

Daisy laughed. "Gotta be the mother of the groom. Her little Nicky knocked up the neighborhood party girl. It's a mom's worst nightmare, at least until the baby arrives. Followed quickly by a nasty divorce and hellacious custody battle."

"Omigod! Look!" said Mel. They both sat up as a paunchy Elvis impersonator waddled through the crush of relatives on the dance floor. This was definitely Las Vegas jumpsuit-and-cape Elvis, not young sexy Memphis Elvis. Mel eased Daisy off his chest. "C'mon!"

"What?" asked Daisy.

"They're about to play our song!"

"What?"

"Trust me. This dance is ours." Daisy sighed as Mel pulled her up. They blended into the crowd and edged onto the dance floor just as Elvis was finishing his stand-up routine in front of the newlyweds.

"...and do you Nicky promise your new bride, Mrs. Tina Tagliagamba that you'll love her tender, you'll treat her nice, you'll put her suspicious mind at ease because you won't be cruel? You'll forever be her big hunk o' love and she'll be your teddy bear? So, neither of you will be lonesome tonight or any night? Answer quick, because..." Elvis paused so the crowd could join him. "It's now or never!"

Nicky looked askance at the groomsmen who had set this up. They were giggling as they saluted him with their plastic champagne flutes. "Yeah, sure, I guess," said Nicky.

"Well then tutti frutti, aw rooti!" shouted the late King of Rock. Then he cut in front of the groom, dipped the bride, and gave her a dramatic albeit brief smooch. Before a shocked Nicky could react, Elvis spun Tina back up and into his arms, and said to the crowd, "There'll be no 'Cryin' in the Chapel' at THIS wedding!" Then he pointed at the keyboard player, who nodded at the bass player and drummer. Mel pulled Daisy onto the dance floor and snuggled her into a standing embrace as Elvis kicked into the song Mel knew was coming, "Can't Help Falling in Love."

Their bodies configured perfectly, a happy harmony of torsos that moved as one to the semi-melodic wail issued by the Unlicensed Phantasm of the Original Memphis Flash. Mel reveled in her warmth as Daisy pressed her cheek against his, giving herself to the moment. When the song ended, Daisy spun away, hiding her face. Mel thought she might be upset until, without looking back at him, she stuck out her hand. He took it, and she pulled him off the dance floor, away from the picnic blanket toward the edge of the garden.

. . .

Mel was mystified as Daisy pulled him through the wedding garden meadow to a tumbledown gardener's shed. The shed interrupted an ivy-covered rampart that towered over a luxurious bed of hollyhocks and dahlias. Mel thought she was taking him inside the moldy shed. Instead, she pulled him through the flowerbed and then through an impossibly narrow space between the shed and the ivy wall.

A blink of darkness, and then a magical secret garden opened to him. Pink beautybush shrubs with yellow throat flowers set off a bower of roses that arched overhead, shedding a red blush carpet of petals that covered a zany bus bench made of artfully stacked turquoise cinder blocks. A moss-covered five-foot granite garden angel holding a birdbath blessed this garden.

Mel was boggled. He turned and saw Daisy smiling at him. "This is mine," she said. "My garden. My father made this for me. He gave it to me when I was six years old."

"Wow," said Mel. The delicious scent of rich, damp earth sweetened by rose petals was making him woozy. "It's so…it's kind of, I don't know, ummm…perfect. Who takes care of it?"

"Beats me. Someone. Someone who loves it as much as I do. I don't even want to know. I want to believe that Flora takes care of it through magic." He saw her looking at the gray granite angel. Flora. Right.

"Come over here." She used her foot to sweep aside some groundcover and revealed a rough-hewn homemade plaster of Paris plaque. Someone – Daisy's father, Mel was sure – had used a stick to write in the wet plaster. The plaque said,

"Let All Who Come Here Know
That As of March 19, 1992
And Henceforth Now & Forever
This Garden is the Domain of Divine Daisy Davenport,
Goddess of Greenery & the Queen of Queens"

"March 19, 1992. My sixth birthday," said Daisy. "Peanut butter sandwiches, Fritos, Dr. Pepper, and Hostess cupcakes. Everyone was here: me, my dad, and all my imaginary friends, starting with Flora. Let's see, who were the others?" She canted her head toward the sky and read the clouds. "Sally Linda was there. She was my twin sister. And also Sassyfrass, Foofy Woogums, Officer Barker – he was a police dog – and naughty

Mabel Lickerish, who was always getting me into trouble. I blamed everything on her."

"Quite a crowd," said Mel.

Daisy looked at him wryly, without a trace of self-pity. "Young Daisy Davenport: only child, no friends, bookworm, dangerous neighborhood, parents who hated each other and couldn't stop fighting. And all of that vanished when I came here, my queenly domain. Here I was a monarch. Here I was rich in playmates, and beauty. And love."

"Have you ever brought Wolfey here?" The second the words escaped his lips he knew he'd goofed. *Dummy!* First, she looked stricken, then pensive. Finally, she took Mel's hand and led him over to the bench. She swept off the rose petals and they sat together knee to knee. The happy mood had evaporated, replaced by something mournful. Mel had the queasy feeling he was about to get dumped by someone he'd just kissed for the first time.

"When I was a teenager," she began, her voice hushed, "I had this secret wish. I wished that someday someone – some special someone, some boy I liked – would do some big, dumb thing, just for me."

"Like that guy who built the Taj Mahal?"

She looked at him funny. "You, ummm, do know that the Taj Mahal is a mausoleum, right?"

"Okay, forget the Taj Mahal. What I MEANT to say was like…like George Gershwin writing 'Our Love Is Here to Stay' for Paulette Goddard, when she was married to Charlie Chaplin."

"Yes! Just like that."

"Uh huh."

"And like what you did today. For me." She looked at him, her cerulean blue eyes glistening. "You *saw* me, Melvin. You saw me and you put what you saw on canvas. You saw *inside* of me. The great artist Melvin Flack created something that was filled with such passion…such…"

"Love," said Mel, looking at the scatter of rose petals in the grass.

"Yes. Love."

"And now…"

"And now…"

"I guess you've got a, you know, problem."

"I guess I do," said Daisy, casting her eyes on the rose petal carpet. "It never occurred to me that when I finally met the man who was smart enough, talented enough, kind enough, and wild enough to thrill me like you did today, I'd be getting ready to marry somebody else. A man I like very much, but…"

Mel tried to throttle the dizzying mix of emotions that was making his head buzz. *Hadn't she just…didn't she just basically say she loved me? But then, there was that other thing. There's always that other thing…*

"When is the wedding?"

"We're still trying to figure that out. Depends on when Wolfey can book the Milstein Hall of Ocean Life at the New York Museum of Natural History for the reception."

"Uh huh." Mel had no idea what to say. He desperately wanted to ask her if she was happy, because she seemed desperately *unhappy*…or at least conflicted…or something. But he didn't want to sound self-serving, or worse, patronizing. Finally, he said, "Thanks for bringing me here. Sharing it. I'm…it made me happy." Whatever he was trying to do, it failed because she put her head in her hands and started to cry.

"What?" said Mel.

"Everything. Every…goddamn…thing."

Mel watched her sob, and his own eyes misted over. This was his life. This was getting tased by his best friend. This was watching Holcombe Parkes throw his life into a dumpster, getting rousted at 4 a.m. by gun-toting cyborgs, having Roxanna Wetherley pilfer his painting while he just stood there. *It's all going to hell right in front of me and there's not a single thing I can do about it.*

Except be sad, of course. And be with Daisy, as best he could, because she was his, just for this one lovely, terrible, heartbreaking day. And then there was that single word to give him hope. "A man I like very much BUT…" She said 'but.' She did. And that could mean he wasn't a complete idiot to hope.

CHAPTER TWENTY-NINE

October 11. France. Yesterday,

Mel visited his personal Garden of Eden in Giverny. As he strolled the gardens, he kept reminding himself he wasn't dreaming. *I'm here. I'm standing right where he stood, seeing what he saw. He pulled this place down from heaven, so he'd have something to paint, and I'd have a reason to swoon all these decades later.* Mel had spent hours staring at those white water lilies in the murals, but here! Bright orange lilies, honey-gold lilies, and lilies that were blush-red with yellow stamens and leathery green foliage. Giverny was Monet's masterpiece, enchanting as ever, begging to be painted. Oh well, maybe next trip.

And yesterday he'd gotten the tip that had brought him here, to this different garden in the cloister of a repurposed medieval Abbey. He was staring at a near perfect 'inspired by' version of Monet's own Clos Normand Garden, with its signature flower tunnel: great arches of rambling roses above a path framed with orange nasturtiums, red dahlias, and pink peonies, trimmed by deep blue bearded irises – a sea of them – and bluebells and blue forget-me-nots against yellow tulips.

And the fragrance! He'd been greeted by the tart smell of rich, moist soil. That smell had warmed and settled into the same bold, rich floral perfume he'd enjoyed yesterday: Giverny in bloom, Fall, late morning. This place had something Giverny didn't have: hidden speakers playing an accordion and cello version of "Tango Jalousie."

Four young females bustled about weeding, watering, and digging, directed by an auburn-haired, rosy-cheeked earth mother in her early 50s: the woman Mel had come to see, he was sure. He sidled up to her and stood stock still as she finished waving instructions at her sun-kissed, straw-hatted apprentices. She finally sensed his presence and turned to him, looking up. "Oui? Puis-je vous aider?"

"I'm pretty sure you can," said Mel. "Helen Quimby, right? From Kokomo, Indiana?" Helen started at this, then smiled at a fellow American. Mel smiled back. "I've come here from New York City. Came for one reason."

"Which is?"

"I want to see it." Mel knew that he was in the right place when she didn't ask what *it* was. Instead, she nodded as she took off her gardening gloves.

"Uh huh. And you are?"

Mel looked out over the garden. "Mel Flack, Queens, New York. You made this for the two of them, right?" He waved at the garden, including the cast iron loveseat for two under the center arch.

"Pretty much," she said, smiling. "Blue was their favorite color." *She's willing to dance the dance* thought Mel. Helen looked at him slyly. "Claude and…and…what was that other woman's name?"

Make or break. Mel reached into his inside coat pocket. "This woman." He handed her Monet's charcoal portrait of his beloved, the one with her staring directly at the viewer. "Euphonia Cavendish-Dupree."

Helen stared at the picture for a good ten seconds, then looked up at Mel. "I always wondered when someone would come looking for her. How'd you find me?"

"When I showed this sketch around Giverny I got a know-nothing headshake from everyone I met. Then I ran into the gentleman who runs the town's Impressionist Museum…" He took a card from his coat pocket. "Louis-Ferdinand Darmesteter."

"Louie, of course." She smiled.

"He said to come here and show this to you. That you knew all about this woman, and you'd let me see it. Will you?"

"Let's have dinner tonight. You tell me your story, and I'll tell you mine."

. . .

Mel wasn't surprised that the abandoned abbey-turned-luxury-hotel spa, "L'Hostellerie de L'Abbaye des Ames Perdues," had a first-class gourmet restaurant. Helen had changed into a black tux-collared jumpsuit as straightforward as her manner. Mel let her order the six-course tasting menu for both of them, with asparagus, Bibb lettuce, and herbs grown in the abbey's veggie garden. Then Mel told Helen his story, with pictures. Demolition had fixed Mel up with a clunky, dumpster-rescue first-generation iPhone, banking Monet's Yankee Stadium art in the photo app. Mel knew Helen was his, the moment he showed her the outfield haystack in front of the water lily fence. He flicked through the rest of the trove, then opened iBooks and let her read a digital copy of Monet's journal as he finished his Foie de Veau à la Lyonnaise. "I'm trying to find out what happened to Euphonia. And I'm betting your story has something to do with that."

"It does indeed," said Helen. "This is a puzzle with two pieces, and I'm happy to say that yours fits snugly with mine." Helen sipped the last of her Pinot Noir, gave her glass to the waiter, and looked at Mel. "In 1993, I was in New York, the 'wonder girl' of the Woolsey Hospitality Group; they own this place and seventy-one other hotels. That's when my husband dumped me."

"Ouch."

"My fault for marrying an actor. Quentin was right at that dream-killing age when he knew he'd never do more than carry a spear. He was playing the Earl of Kent in a bus-and-truck King Lear when 22-year-old Cordelia swept him off his feet. An intermission quickie became true love, or so he thought."

"Cordelia has since moved on?"

"Of course. But not before his majesty the Earl gave me the heave-ho. I'd supported this guy since we met at Yale Drama School, and…" She looked at Mel. "I'm betting you're divorced. Am I right?"

"It's that obvious, huh?"

"Well…"

"Yeah," said Mel. "Sucks."

"Well, it does, and it doesn't," said Helen. "When I stopped weeping, I discovered I'd never really been in love with 'Q' at all. I was just in a kind of…kind of…"

"A rat's nest of toxic neediness," said Mel.

She laughed. "Wow, you HAVE been divorced." They were fast friends, becoming co-conspirators. "When I heard that Woolsey was looking to buy up eccentric heritage properties in Europe and turn them into high-end destination resort hotels, I raised my hand."

"Sounds like a fun job."

"You betcha. When I left New York, I left everything behind, including the old me," said Helen. "Without my hubby, I was a different person. Less crazy, more generous, kinder, and…I guess you could say I stopped fighting the world and started loving it. I mean, France! What's not to love?"

Now they both laughed. "So, this place," prompted Mel.

"You know the story here?"

"Tell me."

As the waiter delivered their lavender crème brûlée, she stage-whispered the backstory. "Built in the 12th century by monks as a sanctuary for sacred virgins. One day a wealthy countess, Antoinette of Neaufles-Saint-Martin, shows up to mourn the death of her husband. She gets herself elected Abbess of the convent and quickly gets bored with all this chastity jazz. She and her more free-thinking acolytes turn this place into a very lucrative high-end brothel for the local noblemen."

"I'm assuming it's honeycombed with secret passageways known only to the lusty fun-seekers," said Mel.

"Of course. At some point the Cardinal catches on and shuts it down. Abandoned for three centuries when some Franciscan nuns move in. They run it from 1910 to 1967, when it's abandoned again. I show up in '93 and it's just what I'm looking for. Amazing backstory, great bones, fire-sale price."

"And so, you buy it and start poking around," said Mel, savoring the last crunch of sugar crust, "and that's when you find it."

Helen stared off, enraptured by the memory. "I was in this junk room filled with stuff the nuns didn't bother to cart away. Behind the hymnbooks and wimples and winter coats was a canvas turned toward the wall. I picked it up, flipped it around…" She seemed to be staring at it, arms-length, suspended in space in front of her.

"Yes?"

Helen turned back to Mel, her voice lush with emotion. "I was looking at love, Mel. The thing was a mess after fifty years in a storeroom, but it didn't make a bit of difference. Pure love, unfiltered, by a man who knew how to put love on canvas. I looked at that picture and it looked back at me with such tenderness that it…oh, I don't know…"

"Jumped off the canvas, took you in its arms, seduced you?"

"Yes, exactly that!"

"That's in the journal. That's what Euphonia said to Monet about his 'Women in the Garden.' That's when he fell in love with her."

Helen nodded. "That look in her eyes. That's what got me. Innocence, vulnerability, and a desperate longing to be wanted, loved, cherished. That's what Monet captured. That's when I knew what love was for the first time."

"So, umm, can I see it?"

She wadded her napkin and plopped it on the table in front of her. "Yes. I think it's time."

CHAPTER THIRTY

Helen tapped a decorative button of the right side of the ten-foot mirror fronting the triple armoire in her office, popping it open. Mel followed Helen into the armoire and out the back panel doorway, down a winding twenty-foot staircase of dusty oak planks and into the musty catacombs. He trailed her through the dank man-made cavern until they came to a peaked doorway with a fire-dragon knocker. "Antoinette's bedchamber. Close your eyes." Mel did as he was told and let Helen pull him into the room, which smelled of sandalwood incense. "Okay. You can open them now."

Mel was standing in a primitive boudoir – Helen's, he was sure – lit by a hundred votive candles. Tie-dyed tapestries in Monet's vivid Giverny palette covered three rock walls and billowed from the ceiling. Mel's eyes moved to the wall opposite the lovers' rose-tufted dream of a queen bed, and there it was: Monet's Euphonia, the day she walked into his life. The missing Monet.

The Mel that stared at Monet's wind-swept beloved, in the billowy white crinoline dress with the emerald bonnet and parasol, was different from the Mel that had spent so many hours staring at Monet's original with Camille. That younger Mel was a besotted spectator, ravaged by envy. Now he knew this work from the inside. He'd used it to paint the love he felt for Daisy, coached by the master himself. He was free to bask in the love that lit this work from within, that had so enchanted Helen. Mel stood there gazing at it as Helen told the story.

"I was in shock when I first saw it. What the hell was I looking at? There was Monet's sig on the bottom, but, I mean, really? Here, in a trash pile? I called Monsieur Darmesteter. When he saw it, he shrieked with joy, hugged me, and danced me around the room. A miracle! But how? He swore me to secrecy as he carried it off for cleanup and restoration. He was going to ask about Euphonia in Giverny, and I was supposed to find out what I could at the abbey. There was a rotting stack of bankers' boxes behind the refectory. That's where I found Euphonia's file."

"Do you happen to have…"

"I do." She nodded and motioned for Mel to sit on the bed. She pulled a fat file from the bottom drawer of the nightstand, opened it, and placed an item between them. It was Monet's hand-drawn wedding invitation on cottony homemade card stock. He'd sketched his bride's smiling face framed by a modest veil. He was behind her, wide-eyed and smitten. Mel's French had gotten better:

Claude & Euphonia Invite you to Celebrate
as Two Souls Become One Forever
Love, Laughter, Music, Dancing, Food.
September 3, 1924
From 2 p.m. till the End of Time.

"Love is the emblem of eternity: it confounds all notion of time, effaces all memory of a beginning, all fear of an end."
Germaine De Stael

"They were married?"

"Well, sort of," said Helen. "Louie found the great-grandson of Monet's majordomo Max who kept the records of the estate: comings and goings, expenses, stuff like that. Monet was heartbroken when he came back from New York. Then Euphonia shocked him by returning in May

1922. The old man came alive again. The ceremony was a non-legally binding whoop-de-do hosted by Georges Clemenceau and attended by townspeople. I actually found a photo..." Mel expected a stiff wedding portrait, or maybe the happy couple doing a sedate waltz. Instead, Mel gazed at a venerable boulevardier roguishly dipping Euphonia in what looked like a tango move.

"The tango?" said Mel.

"Monet was wild about it, and so was Euphonia. I think that's what kept a chain-smoking, arthritic, wine-loving workaholic alive."

"Until…"

"December 5, 1926. That garden where we met? That's my nod to the one in Giverny where Monet and Euphonia spent their last year together, sitting on a bench, holding hands. She was the one Monet wanted with him on his deathbed, but the moment he died the hammer came down. Euphonia had gotten sideways with Blanche Hoschede-Monet, Claude's stepdaughter, and heir to his fortune. Blanche literally threw Euphonia into the street. Turned her away from the funeral, snubbed her at the burial, scrubbed every trace of her from Giverny. That's why Euphonia showed up here."

She handed Mel another plastic sleeve. "One more." Mel guessed right: Euphonia's death certificate. December 5, 1927, the one-year anniversary of Monet's death. "Says she died of rheumatic heart failure, but I'm pretty sure it was stress cardiomyopathy."

"A broken heart."

"Right."

"Do you know what happened to her money?"

"She gave it to the French Catholic Church, for a new mission to care for lepers on the island of Molokai in Hawaii."

Mel stood and walked up to the painting, staring at Euphonia's face. There was something singular about it, something he'd been trying to name. Then it clicked. *Renoir*, Mel thought. Monet usually hid the faces of his models. Here he'd captured Euphonia's face with the lush, pearly-smooth rose tints of Renoir's late portraits, and the face took the "golden time" light perfectly. He banked the colors and textures for the finish of his Daisy portrait. "So beautiful," said Helen.

"And sad," said Mel.

"Sad?" Helen was surprised. "Why sad?"

Mel turned to her, surprised by her surprise. "Well, I mean...ummm... losing him killed her."

Helen stood and faced the portrait with him. "There's no death in that picture. There's just love. Pure happiness."

"And to have the talent to capture that love," said Mel "I can feel how happy Monet was painting this."

"How many people ever know that kind of love, even for a single moment? She and Monet had it for three glorious years." She turned to Mel, smiled, and took his hand. "That's why we meet here once a week."

Mel blinked. "We? You mean you and..."

"Louie." Helen turned back to the portrait. "We sit in the garden. We hold hands. We enjoy a glass of wine. We dance the tango. Then we come down here and make love under the benevolent gaze of Euphonia Cavendish-Dupree. And it makes us both so happy. True love, at last."

Of course. The garden, the bench, the boudoir: it wasn't for Claude and Euphonia, it was for Helen and Louie. "Thanks so much for bringing me here, showing it to me," said Mel. He took out his smartphone and started to take a picture. She put her hand on his arm and he paused.

"You're the third living party who knows about this. I know we can't keep this secret forever, but..."

"I'll do what I can. I'm pretty sure it won't be a problem." She pulled her hand back, and he captured Euphonia's portrait, then looked at the screen. *Perfect happiness captured perfectly.* "Can I grab the wedding invite? And the death certificate too?" Helen nodded. Mel clicked off the wedding invite, but when he tried to shoot the death certificate through the sleeve, the glassy plastic mirrored his image and obscured the document. Mel pulled the certificate out of the sleeve...and a wrinkled, nut-brown bit of parchment, brittle as a butterfly wing, floated to the floor. Mel picked it up and read:

A: Monsieur Max Dumont, pour C. Monet
Le facture de service compris
14 février 1925
45 francs
Daphne LeClerc
La Sage-femme

Mel blinked, then blinked again. Helen was busy returning the other documents to Euphonia's folder. Mel quickly snapped a picture of the fragile scrap and slid it back behind the death certificate in the sleeve.

"Are you okay?"

Mel saw Helen staring at him. His burning brain had set his face on fire. "Fine, fine."

"Are you sure?"

"Really. Wonderful, actually," said Mel. "Just, I don't know, overwhelmed by seeing all this. Wow." She turned back to tidying up as Mel tried to remember what Demo had taught him about the smartphone texting function. He pulled up Madame LeClerc's bill, selected Demo's email address and typed:

Demo – This was hiding in Euphonia's stuff. Grab Sam, figure out if this is what I think it is. Holding my breath. Yer pal Mel.

CHAPTER THIRTY-ONE

October 14
Surrogate's Court, Bronx County Public Administration Building
9:47 a.m.

"Your Honor, thank you for this opportunity to right a terrible wrong and deliver one of the great discoveries in art history to its legal, deserved owners."

Mel watched Harriet Tubman Foster stand at the podium and deliver her opening remarks to Judge Lafcadio Banks, a dumpy, bald, black-robed troll with the baleful demeanor of a hangman. Foster was a runway-model gorgeous African American legal advocate for the New York City Housing Authority, and by extension the Metropolitan Museum of Art and Holcombe Parkes. Holcombe was sitting between Chase Hancock and Melissa Colfax, the Bronx City Council member eager to brag about the jobs Parkes Place would bring to her district. The fourteen paintings Mel had pulled from the wall were perched on mahogany easels, arranged in a three-quarters semicircle angled so everyone could see them.

Harriet picked up a thick sheaf of alligator-clipped papers. "I hold in my hand city documents, certified and notarized, that chronicle the ownership history of the Ziegler-Haversham Building. This provides incontrovertible evidence that the building was abandoned by its last official owners in 1988, with the title reverting by default to the New York City Housing Authority."

Mel squirmed in the twelve dollar, just-slightly-too-big charcoal-gray herringbone suit Demo had forced on him at the Bronx Goodwill Store. He hadn't worn a suit since he'd bailed on the ad biz twenty-six years ago. He'd forgotten how much a (two-dollar, red paisley, Ralph Lauren) necktie felt like a noose.

Harriet turned and stared at Mel. "Melvin Flack, a homeless, trespassing drifter wantonly vandalized a wall in said building, stealing the property of the New York City Housing Authority, and thus robbing the citizens of the great state of New York."

Mel felt everyone's eyes burn into him. He turned and checked the gallery for the fifth time that morning. Velocity was here with Demolition, both clad in chinos and collared shirts as if dressed for a semi-formal dumpster dive. Simon Brittle chatted up Edison Ziff. Still no Wolfey, and no Sam Dollar. *Where are you, Sam? Need you, buddy.*

"The property – this astonishing trove of work from the hand of Impressionist legend Claude Monet, displayed here before you today – belongs to all of us. There is absolutely no reason – none whatsoever – for this court to reward vandalism and larceny."

Mel stared at the Judge. The words of Daisy echoed in his ears. *"Lafcadio Banks, judicial lifer. Appointed by his fellow Dartmouth alumnus Nelson Rockefeller in '72. Bad news? Well known for hoisting martinis with Nancy and Ronnie at White House Sound of Music sing-alongs. Good news? Just hoisted a flute of bubbly at his only daughter's big fat gay wedding at the couple's Sustainable Food Collective in Bennington, Vermont. Cranky, skeptical but persuadable…maybe."*

Harriet summed up her argument for the Judge. "This case is as one-sided as a hanging, Your Honor. If my worthy adversaries have a shred of integrity, we can wrap this up by noon. The law is with the people of New York City – completely, unconditionally, unequivocally – and the other side is savvy enough to know it. The city owned the building when the art was found, and so it owns the paintings. Everything else that's said in this hearing, if I may employ a colloquialism, is just so much chin music."

Harriet sat, and Judge Banks nodded to Daisy, who stood and walked to the podium. Something was different about her, but what? Then it clicked. Mel was accustomed to seeing her in "serious as a heart attack black." Now – in court! – she was dressed in a sassy jade green jacket with floral accents, a lacy white blouse, and a knee-length tangerine skirt. She wasn't dressed for the funeral; she was dressed for the *party*. He realized his mouth was open, and he clamped it shut as he continued to stare at her.

"Your Honor, thank you for the opportunity to advocate for my client, Mister Melvin Flack and his friends in the Moist Robots art collective. They assert themselves as rightful owners of this astonishing trove of art with two compelling arguments. The first is a fact that is, to echo Ms. Foster, complete, unconditional, and unequivocal." She turned and smiled and Mel. "If this art had not been discovered by my client, Melvin Durward Flack, we wouldn't be here. The art would still be in that wall, turning to dust." She pointed to the paintings. "The city owned that building by default for twenty-nine years and made no effort to rescue these great works. Pure negligence, bordering on the criminal. Therefore, he and his friends have a preemptive claim on them."

He felt those familiar butterflies in his chest as he watched her. It was something different than mere adoration. What was it? Yes. *Enchantment.* He marveled at the idiotic jinx of love: how something so improbable, hopeless, and certain to end badly could generate such *euphoria…*

"Our second argument involves legal precedent," said Daisy. "We will show how courts in the recent past have awarded paintings like these here before you to people who assumed stewardship through innocent happenstance."

"Innocent happenstance? That stuff was stolen! RIPPED OFF!" Everyone turned to a red-faced Holcombe Parkes, who was leaning over the railing of the gallery.

The Judge pounded his gavel. "Mister Parkes, this is a formal legal proceeding, not your luxury box at a Las Vegas prize fight. Please refrain from obnoxious grandstanding behaviors."

Holcombe had his mouth open ready to apologize when Daisy muttered "Good luck with that."

He glared at her and started to object but saw the Judge smiling at her. He phumphered, "Ummm, yes, right, your Honor. Sorry."

Daisy checked her notes, then looked up at the Judge. "With your indulgence, I'd like to assert one additional non-legal basis to award these paintings to Mister Flack that supports the other two. That's future intention. Mister Flack and his friends will not sell these paintings or hide them away. They plan to share them with the people of New York City and the world just as Ms. Foster's group intends. Only our group will present them in a distinctive way much different from the other claimant in this case. Thank you."

CHAPTER THIRTY-TWO

Daisy had assured Mel that the Claude Squad would know its fate quickly, and Harriet wasted no time buttressing her one and only (strong) argument. The formidable Leland van der Kellen, New York City's foremost expert in property law, took the stand and rolled out precedent after precedent, ending with an especially nasty swipe at Mel. "The law is crystal clear," said van der Kellen. "It states that by removing these paintings, Mister Flack looted a publicly-owned building the way the Kunstschutz plundered Europe for the Hitler Gang in World War 2."

Daisy countered by bringing on her own expert: Simon Brittle. Simon regaled the court with the rollicking yarn of Guido Lanzetti, "the world's luckiest gardener." The story began with thieves stealing Gauguin's 'Harlequin Mask and Mandolin' from a private collector, then hopping a train for their getaway. The cops were in hot pursuit, so the thieves ditched the painting and fled. The railroad had no idea what it had, and so peddled the masterpiece at its yearly auction for abandoned goods. "Our Mister Lanzetti bought the Gauguin for forty-five thousand lira – about thirty-two bucks – and hung it on the wall of his kitchen for forty-four years," said Simon. "His son eventually got married, and the new bride sparked to what they had. Whole thing ended in court, the original owner suing Lanzetti."

"And what was the verdict?" asked Daisy.

Brittle grinned at Judge Banks. "This Judge ruled that Guido had bought the painting in good faith and proved a worthy steward for forty-four years. He gave it to Lanzetti."

"Do you believe," asked Daisy, "that that case sets a precedent for this one?"

"You betcha!" said Simon. "Melvin got a lucky break when he found this stuff, no question. He coulda done anything with these pictures: burned 'em, put 'em up in his kitchen, sold 'em on Ebay, or stashed 'em in a hidey-hole of his own. What did he do? He put all but one of 'em in the hands of Ed Ziff, world-class preservation expert. And the other one he brought into the Met so we could look it over. Vandalism? Not. Larceny? Are you kiddin' me? City of New York oughta be givin' Melvin a ticker tape parade instead of kicking him to the curb."

As Simon returned to his seat, Harriet Tubman Foster stood. "Your Honor, you've now heard our two arguments. I'd be willing to put the question of who gets these paintings to you now. However, Ms. Hudnutt-Parkes brought up the issue of intent. As it's not even noon yet, would you permit us to address this? This strengthens our case even more." The Judge nodded.

Harriet called Council member Melissa Colfax. She praised the entrepreneurial genius of her friend Holcombe Parkes and raved about the thousands of new jobs this "visionary alliance" of government, art, and private enterprise would bring to the Bronx in the form of "Parkes Place," a 'breakthrough' multi-use casino/hotel/condo-MAXIUM development. Colfax was followed by Chase Hancock, who spoke (a little too) glowingly of munificent civic benefactor Holcombe Parkes. As he spoke, minions clad in metallic gold "HolParksDevCorp" jumpsuits placed dignified renderings of the Met's new one hundred ten-million-dollar Holcombe Parkes/Claude Monet Discovery Gallery on a new set of easels.

And then, finally, Holcombe Parkes presented himself. His underlings replaced the Met art with the heinously gaudy "Parkes Place" promotional stuff that had turned Mel's stomach the night he was evicted from the Love Shack. "One hundred and ten million dollars is a lot of money to donate for a new gallery in the Metropolitan Museum of Art," said an emphatic Parkes. "It shows you that I…mean…*business*." He walked over to the Parkes-branded development art. "Millions of people from all the over the world are going to come here to look at this art, to dine, to stay a night, to gamble, and then, perhaps, to make this great place their new home." Parkes turned to Daisy and Mel. "This is what we're doing with Monet's stuff. What's your plan? You got something? Now's the time to let us see it. If you don't, well…" He smiled at Melissa and Chase, nodded to the Judge, and sat back down.

"Ms. Hudnutt-Parkes?"

Daisy took a deep breath, picked up her legal pad and started to rise. Mel put his hand on her forearm. She stopped, startled, and looked a question at him. "What are you doing?" she whispered.

"I got this," smiled Mel.

"But I..".

"Please."

They held each other's eyes for a long moment. Then Daisy gave him a single nod and sat back down. Mel marveled at how much had changed since they'd met. He was no longer the hapless butt of God's cosmic joke. She was no longer the ferocious black-clad go-it-alone legal avenger. Mel picked up Monet's journal and positioned himself at the axis of the two art exhibits: Monet to his left, Parkes Place to his right. He turned to the Judge. "Your Honor, Mr. Parkes asked if we had any concept art that would show the court how we planned to showcase these paintings. We do. Everyone here has been staring at it the whole time." Mel turned to Parkes. "Look, it's right here, Holcombe." He moved in front of the Monet paintings.

"Yes!" shouted Velocity. The Judge looked at her and raised his gavel. She crouched back in her chair and dragged her thumb and index finger across her lips in an "I'm zipping it" gesture.

Mel turned to the paintings. "What was Monet's dream? It was so much more than just creating another art gallery. It was – is – to create a new *kind* of place. He painted the place he wants. More importantly, Monet *told us* what he wants, in *his own words*, and I can't improve on them." Mel flipped open the journal to the page with the marker ribbon. "May I quote Monsieur Monet?"

"Please," said the Judge.

Mel read words that were so familiar, they'd become a part of him. *"I have in mind a new kind of place: one that will metamorphose the very nature of art itself! No longer something to stare at, the work here will offer art-lovers something they can step into and live inside! Three-dimensional, immersive, delighting the senses and stimulating the emotions! All my great themes and inspirations presented as living theater, with my patrons joining me inside the dream of ever-evolving creative inspiration!"*

"Excuse me," interrupted Harriet Foster. "Are you saying...is your plan to, actually, what, get the New York Yankees to put haystacks in their outfield? Turn the infield into a koi pond? Really?"

"Of course not," said Mel. "Let me complete Monsieur Monet's statement of his ambitions." He turned back to the diary. *" 'It will redefine the nature of the art museum, from a dank, passive catacomb to a sun-washed, open-air living experience that invites everyone to pick up a brush and find the Monet in themselves!' "*

Mel let that phrase echo in the room for a moment. "This has nothing to do with the real Yankee Stadium. It has everything to do with being an artist, about the joy of creating something new, unique, and inspirational. Monet wants a place as different from that..." Mel pointed to the Parkes Place "casino-condo project, "...as a Ferrari is from a plow horse, as Disneyland is from a video arcade, as...as..." Mel moved to Monet's painting of the outfield fence water lilies reflected in the warning track pond. "As his Yankee Stadium is from just another casino. We have a site all picked out: a heritage ballpark perfect for Monet's dream field."

Mel closed the diary and stepped forward till he was directly in front of Judge Banks. "That's our case. It's not about money. It's about the intention of a great artist to inspire the world. What I've learned..." Mel paused and looked at Daisy. He wanted to get this right. "Finding these artworks and reading Monsieur Monet's journal have changed me, your Honor. Claude Monet was filled with joy when he created these paintings. He wanted to design and build a place to share that joy: the joy of art. He doesn't want us to admire his work. He wants us to be inside a place so full of beauty that we will have no choice but to create beautiful things ourselves. We can do it, Judge! But not without your help. Now it's up to you. Only you can make his – and our – dream come true."

CHAPTER THIRTY-THREE

1 p.m.

The Claude Squad huddled on the courtroom steps for lunch, munching tomato-cucumber sandwiches on onion cornbread, with a side of curried chickpea salad. Daisy suggested a coffee run, prompting Demo to shout, "Death before Starbucks!" As they sipped their artisanal java jolts from "Giddy Up!" the group split down the middle on their chances. Velocity and Demo were in for the win, with Daisy and Edison Ziff reluctantly voting thumbs down because of the dour, conservative Judge. Simon Brittle demurred, preferring to gaze at the "shimmering clouds" overhead, as rhapsodized by Billie Holiday in her rendition of "Autumn in New York." Mel pretended to listen to this debate, but all he could think of was, *where is Sam?*

· · ·

Back in court. Judge Banks looked at his notes, then at the litigants. "I am sympathetic to the cause of the so-called 'Claude Squad'."

"Shit," whispered Daisy without turning her head. "We're dead." Mel blanched. *Is this it? Really?*

"Were this an arbitration hearing and I had a free hand to dole out these masterworks of art as I saw fit, I might very well award them to Mister Flack and his associates." Mel turned his head. Holcombe Parkes couldn't help himself. He broke out in a broad grin and held his open palm up for a high-five from Harriet Foster. She ignored him. "However, I must acknowledge that Ms. Foster was accurate in her opening statement. The city of New York did in fact own, by default, the building where this art was discovered, and every tenet of the law dictates that the city so owned the paintings. I therefore rule…"

The courthouse doors burst open. Everyone turned. A lightning bolt of adrenaline hit Mel, like the one he'd felt when he'd first unfurled that roll of paintings and saw Monet's signature scrawl. Sam Dollar! At last! "Am I in time? Have you handed down a decision, your Honor?" Sam was dressed as a third Blues Brother: Ray Ban Wayfarer shades, rumpled suit, and skinny black necktie. He was holding a file folder.

The Judge was vexed. "I was, in fact, just on the verge of doing just that. I was about to award these works to…"

"STOP!" said Sam.

"This Court hasn't recognized you, Mister…"

"Sam Dollar, your Honor. I'm one of the Claude Squad, and I tender my deepest, most profound apologies, but…well…I have evidence in my possession that changes everything." He had everyone's attention, and he knew it. He surveyed the courtroom like a seasoned barrister. "I believe I can now prove, beyond a shadow of a doubt, that the only acknowledged owner of these paintings, Euphonia Cavendish-Dupree, has a direct heir. An heir who is alive today and is therefore the legal owner of these works."

Both Harriet Foster and Daisy jumped to their feet. "Your Honor," said Harriet, "this kind of ridiculous side show may pass muster on television, but it has no place…"

Judge Banks held his hand up, then looked at Sam. "Evidence? With you?"

Sam nodded at the Judge, then angled himself so he could address the court, both legal teams and the gallery. "Let me begin with this." He handed the Judge a piece of paper. "That's the only document I'll present that isn't original, your Honor. That's a copy of what Mr. Flack texted me on his recent journey to France." Sam looked toward Mel.

"Ummm, yes, your Honor," said Mel, standing. "My investigation into the fate of the owner of these works, Ms. Cavendish-Dupree led me to a hotel…that is, it's a hotel now, it used to be a convent. Anyway, it seems Ms. Cavendish-Dupree went there in 1927 to mourn the death of her lover, Monsieur Monet. The woman who ran this hotel was a sort of the de facto historian of the place. She had a file on the life of Euphonia. That piece of paper came from her file. It had been overlooked."

"It's in French," said the Judge.

"Mr. Flack speaks French," said Sam.

"A little," said Mel. "Enough." Sam grabbed the paper from the Judge and walked it over to Mel.

Mel knew what it said, but pretended he was seeing it for the first time. "It says…let's see…'To Max Dumont, representing Claude Monet. Bill for services rendered, February 14, 1925, 45 francs. Signed Daphne LeClerc…" Mel looked up at the gallery to deliver the punchline. "Mid-wife."

A long moment of silence as this echoed in the courtroom. "Mid-wife?" said the Judge.

"My first thought, your Honor," said Mel. "Why would Claude Monet need the services of a mid-wife in 1925?"

"And so, he sent it to me," said Sam. "And I have devoted every minute of every hour since then trying to find out what bearing it has on the matter of these paintings. And I believe I've discovered the truth." He opened his file folder. "Anyone here ever heard of the 'Bronx Reliquary of Cultural History'?" Blank stares. "Run by a pal of mine, crazy guy named Doyle Blackwood. He has made it his business to rescue and preserve Bronx history, in the form of paper documents purged by institutions from city government to civic organizations to newspapers to libraries to museums. He has a warehouse full of files…including the records of the Bronx Women's Art League."

"The Bronx…" Mel blurted the words without thinking. Sam smiled and nodded.

"Depression put it out of business in 1931," continued Sam. "All the files went to the New York Historical Society, which got rid of them seven years ago, which is when Doyle got his hands on them. Big file for Euphonia, of course, but that's not this one." Sam held a file over his head, then brought it down and began laying documents on the Judge's desk. "This one belonged to Euphonia's best friend, fellow trustee and soulmate. What I'm placing before you are all originals." Sam put one document after another in front of the Judge. "Birth certificate...naturalization papers...and adoption papers. All for a male child born on February 14, 1925, in Giverny, France to Euphonia Cavendish-Dupree, no father listed."

"This person would be ninety-one years old," said the Judge.

"That's right," said Sam. "And I'd like you to indulge me, your Honor. I will reveal the name of the heir after I present one additional document." He pulled an ancient envelope out of this file. Once ivory, it had aged into a mottled caramel color. Sam removed the letter, just slightly less faded. "Mel? Can I get you to read this? It's in French, but..."

Mel stared for a moment. *Me? Why me?* Then he got up and took the letter from Sam. *"My dearest, darling Jean."* Mel turned to Sam. "Jean?"

"Jean. After Monet's first son, with Camille," said Sam. "Keep reading, buddy."

Mel looked down at the page. *"These are the saddest words that can be written: I am your mother, and yet you do not know me."* Mel paused, gathering himself. *"If you are reading this, then you've discovered the sordid history of your birth and abandonment. I don't blame you if you hate me. How could any mother do the monstrous thing I've done, shattering the most sacred bond life offers, that of mother and child? My defense is paltry. It is that once, I myself knew a perfect love: a literal bonding of souls, pure happiness, a love so great it lifted me to the heavens. My life had been a hellish thing till I found this bond. When my great love – your father – died, I found myself pulled downward into a..."* Mel stared at the word, then looked up. "Tourbillon?"

"Whirlpool," said Chase Hancock.

Mel nodded. *"....whirlpool of grief. I had no thoughts except those that demanded self-murder. For both of us to survive, I had to renounce the world I'd known: the world of greed, lust, vanity, deceit, and hatred. To live, I had to die into a new, better world of ministration to the hopeless and helpless. And to do this, I had to surrender you to the loving care of one who would love* you as I so wanted to, but couldn't. I don't know why God has visited this unbearable grief that is crushing me. My only wish is that someday you find a way to forgive me, and this forgiveness makes you happy. If nothing else, know that you are loved: by God, by the angels, and by your bereft mother. All blessings, dearest. Yours forever, Euphonia Cavendish-Dupree."

"Wow," said Velocity. "That's epic."

"So, who is the heir? Are you certain this person is still alive?" said the Judge.

"Absolutely, your Honor. In fact,…" Sam paused, reveling in his moment in the spotlight. "… he's right here in this very courtroom. The name on this file is Louella "Lolly" Brittle. And the heir is her son, Jean…now known as Simon."

A blast wave of silence stunned the courtroom. Then, all at once, everyone turned on a wide-eyed Simon. "But I," he stuttered. "She…she never…there's no way that…."

"Think, Simon," said Sam. Simon closed his mouth, and Mel could see his friend vaulting back through his entire lifetime, putting the whole thing together in a brand-new way. Mel joined him, remembering those Friday afternoon lunches in the Met's Kravis Wing Dining Room, with Simon regaling him with tales of the "mother" who was more of an eccentric aunt, treating her "boy" like a combination favored valet/male consort. *"I did pretty well with you for someone with no maternal instincts whatsoever." Omigod*, thought. *It's true. It makes perfect sense.*

Mel stood up along with Velocity, Daisy, Demo and Edison Ziff. They joined Sam in surrounding their friend. A dazed Simon struggled to his feet and let Velocity wrap him in a joyous bear hug. Then, one by one, everyone hugged him, ending with Mel. Simon whispered in his ear, "Hot damn, genius. I guess this means we win."

"I guess so, my friend."

CHAPTER THIRTY-FOUR

October 15, 12:53 a.m.
Carole Lombard Grand Salon, Dream Palace, Bronx, N.Y.
Mel was…what was the right word? Drunk? No, not really. He could see and speak with crystal clarity, even after four flutes of vegan champagne. Mel hadn't known there was such a thing, but when Demo produced a case of the stuff purchased on Daisy's credit card, Velocity informed the group that most so-called champagnes and sparkling wines used fining agents, including carmine, made from the bodies of dried cochineal beetles.

Mel decided the right word for his condition was "high," as if he'd washed down a Xanax with a double cappuccino. High, happy, and mellow, with a tiny tinge of melancholy, because he knew this perfect moment would fade to memory in a blink. *Nostalgia for the present.* Yes, that's what he was feeling. He thought of Monet's wonderful journal entry about Coney Island. *"I've never felt so alone and blessed to be so – apart yet animated by the infectious joy of the crowd's shrieking laughter."* Mel knew the feeling: this was his life. In the crowd, yet apart. Observing, like an artist. Trying to see, really *see*.

What did he see now? He saw a giddy, slightly-more-than-tipsy Simon Brittle in a huddle with Sam Dollar and Edison Ziff howling at the cosmic joke that'd been played on him. They were reveling in the moment that Velocity had just captured on her smartphone and posted on YouTube: Holcombe Parkes finally getting what had happened to him. Velocity got

Parkes full-face as he yelled at the Judge. "Are you saying this, this *geezer* gets this stuff? This *flunky*? This *NOBODY? SERIOUSLY?!?*" A jubilant Daisy had then leaned over to Mel. "There's no unkicking his ass this time, is there? I've waited years for this, and the wait was sooooooo worth it."

Mel saw Velocity huddled with her fellow Moist Robots, plotting their next move. The first thing Simon had shouted on the steps of the Courthouse was, "Loyal members of the Claude Squad, an announcement! What's mine is ours! Let's make my ever-lovin' daddy's dream come true!" Could they? Was it even possible? Now they'd have the chance to find out.

And finally, he saw Daisy. She was alone, smiling, sipping champagne, and savoring the moment, leaning beneath a poster of Carole Lombard gleefully socking Frederic March on the chin in the poster for "Nothing Sacred." He glided over to her. "I've got something that belongs to you."

"Oh?"

"Want to see what it is?

"This couldn't possibly be an original treasure from the fabled hand of master artist Melvin Flack, could it?"

"Mmmmmm, possibly."

"Is this the big dumb thing I've longed for my entire life?"

"Nope. It's a small dumb thing. But done with big love."

"I'll be the judge of that. Let's have a look."

· · ·

Mel led Daisy by the hand into the cavernous great chamber of the Dream Palace. The rot and ruin had been cleared, leaving a dank, yawning cavern that smelled of chlorine bleach and made Mel feel like he was inside the belly of a blue whale. A single work light on stage drew them forward until they were on the stage, standing in front of a painting on a wooden easel draped with a beige drop cloth. Mel rolled the work light in position to illuminate his masterpiece. "Ready?"

Daisy put her champagne flute down on the stage, took a deep breath and nodded. "Yes." Mel yanked the cloth, letting it puddle at their feet. Daisy gasped, put her hands to her face, and took a step back. She stared at the painting for a full half a minute. Then she turned to Mel and wrapped him in a bone-crushing hug.

Mel hugged her right back as he looked over her shoulder at his work: the portrait he'd begun that glorious day in the Queens Botanical Garden, now complete. There was Daisy posed on an emerald mound of grass that Mel crafted, as per Monet, with an infinite number of comma-like brush strokes to give it motion. Likewise, the sky, a revelation of feathery white clouds against a dream of bold azure blue. And there was Daisy, so ravishing in her memorable white dress with the emerald trim, veiled bonnet, and parasol. Mel was damn proud of this picture. Claude Monet himself had coached him through its birth, but Mel was the one who hadn't given up or stopped or said "good enough." He worked it and worked it to make it more active, more vivid, more beautiful: especially the face. Mel had studied his cell phone grab of Monet's portrait of Euphonia. Mel had already captured that perfect oval, with the laughing eyes, pert nose, and flirtatious, teasing mouth. After seeing the original of Monet's work, Mel had added just a hint of "Renoir blush" to Daisy's complexion.

Daisy finally released him. She took his hand and stood beside him, gazing at it. "It's...it's..."

"Good?"

She laughed. "It's...wonderful. A long moment of staring. "When I'm gone..."

"Seventy years from now."

"Seventy years from now," she laughed, "I want this to have its own room in the Melvin Flack Wing of the Metropolitan Museum of Art, with a plaque right underneath it."

"That says what?"

"That says, 'Someone once knew me well enough to do this.'"

A shiver of delight raced up Mel's spine. *Whatever happens, it's been worth it.* "Nice. Thanks. It's meant to be a, you know..."

"What?"

"A wedding present."

"Really?" She looked at him in mock surprise. "Who's getting married?"

YES!!! Mel stifled the urge to whoop in ecstasy. *Breathe. Don't start babbling. Don't blow it. Play it cool.* "I, ummm, thought you and Wolfey…"

The smallest Mona Lisa smile played on her lips as continued to stare at the picture. "I broke it off. Something happened."

"What?"

Daisy pointed at the picture. "That." Then she turned to Mel. "You." Mel felt the urge to whoop again and squelched it as she continued. "Wolfey is a lovely man. Kind, generous. He was offering me a nice, safe, thoroughly pleasant cocktail party of a life. I was sure I wanted that life until things changed, and I realized I wanted something more. Something, I don't know…"

"I know."

"You do?"

Mel put his finger to her lips to shush her. He held out his hand and led her off the stage through the darkness to the center of the theater. Then he tilted his head up and shouted, "SHOW ME THE MONET!"

In an instant, night became day. The entire whale belly exploded with blinding white light. Then Daisy gasped as the walls around her begin to *melt*. What had seemed real – walls, ceiling, portals – dissolved, and a derelict Bronx movie palace became an iconic sun-drenched garden in France. The six digital high-def projectors Demo and his Moist Robot friends had rigged that very evening turned the crash pad of the Moist Robots into a three-dimensional, augmented-reality version of Monet's magnificent garden at Giverny: not the real garden, but Monet's shimmering Impressionist *dream* of his garden. Daisy and Mel were alive inside this bright, vivid dream which was itself alive. Bees darted, danced, and hovered. A milion radiant flowers shivered and glistened with dew drops as the limbs of willow trees swayed in the morning breeze. Somewhere a cello sextet played "Our Love Is Here to Stay."

"Here's the 'something more,' Daisy. Here's the *big* dumb thing I promised." She turned to him, took his hands, and looked in his eyes. Mel melted. He was hers. "It's a garden, Daisy, the one you were born to create, and I was born to paint." Mel saw it on her face: the thing that artists live to create. *Astonishment.* She was astonished. "Funny. The big lesson of this past month…the thing that Monet taught me…is that painting isn't some big deal. It's nothing more than capturing and communicating love. With the two of us working in your garden, we can do what Monet did. We can make the world fall in love with itself."

That look on her face: where had he seen it before? Oh yes, of course: the pure elation he'd seen so long ago on the face of that sixteen-year-old Puerto Rican girl on her wedding day. He looked into her beautiful blue eyes. "You are filled with joy, Divine Daisy Davenport. The world *needs* that joy, and I am ready to throw it on canvas and share it with the world, for the pure fun of it." She took a half step forward and kissed him: a warm, wet, tear-filled kiss that ignited swirls of ecstasy in every cell of his body. The kiss went on and on, longer and longer, deeper and deeper, and Mel breathed it in. He banked every moment in three dimensions because he knew he'd never be this happy again, because nobody could ever be this happy again.

EPILOGUE

One Year, Eight Months, Eleven Days Later (July 12)

Melvin Durward Flack knew his light would vanish in seconds. *One more push! You can do it! NOW!* But he couldn't, not this evening. He was too busy basking in the mundane splendor of this perfect, perfectly ordinary moment to care.

Till now, his "personal exultation" top three moments were:

ONE – The NO That Changed Everything: The day he said NO to Chase Hancock when the Met offered him (what he thought was) his dream job at (what he thought was) his dream salary. So simple – all he had to do was fall backwards into the chasm of his inevitable fate as a failed artist. *Where had that "no" come from?* Somewhere other than his mind, that was for sure. It was completely unlike him...and it was the first moment he was fully himself. In some miraculous way, his soul overrode his brain. And it was the first domino that pushed all the others.

TWO – There's the Cliff! JUMP! Ahhh, that day in the wedding garden with delightful Daisy. Mel was defeated by the moment, ready to give up forever when Claude Monet – the Great Man himself – shamed him, cajoled him, then tutored him. *"Stop thinking! PAINT!"* Those words were the prod he needed. He stopped fretting and got after his task. *How could I not, with my hero yelling at me?* And he hadn't stopped since.

And that moment inspired the revelation in the Secret Garden when Daisy told him that, yes, she felt for him what he felt for her.

THREE: On A Mission from Claude – The moment Mel stood before Judge Lafcadio Banks and let Claude Monet speak for himself. *His* place, done *his* way per *his* instructions. As Mel read Monet's words, he knew why he had found the paintings that fateful day: because it took one to know one, and if Claude was going to get his insanely ambitious "new kind of place," he'd need a fellow artist who was as crazy and committed as he was. And that would be Melvin Durward Flack. And the last miracle, the revelation of Simon's maternity, sealed the deal forever.

But today's exaltation threatened to obliterate this top three, very likely capturing the coveted Number One spot:

RIGHT NOW – Golden Time Near-Sunset, Claude Monet Dream Field, Painting Daisy Planting Flowers.

The late afternoon honey-amber light made the whole garden glow with the luster of stained glass. Daisy was tamping in the last of her fuscia-pink halo hollyhocks on the "island" garden where the pitcher's mound had been. Mel stood at home plate, marveling at the glimmer of Daisy and her blooms mirrored in the waters of the infield koi pond. He'd been trying to capture the moment before it vanished: break it down, imagine it, and get it on canvas. His good-luck thumbnail of his grumpy mentor Monet was alligator-clipped on the bottom right of the frame as always, scolding Mel with his eyes. *"Look! See! Don't think, feel the colors, and paint them! Fall in love with the light and paint the love. Ignore the brain, move the hand!"*

The last spark of direct sunlight on the last yellow rose at the top of the tallest outfield trellis blinked off. *Now what?* Mel grinned. *Now I'll get up at dawn tomorrow, make a cup of coffee, come out here, and start all over again.*

He parked his brush on the easel, put down his palette and turned to stare at the astonishing "dream field" that filled the horizon: the glorious riot of flowers, haystacks, and lily ponds that Monet had summoned from his imagination. Mel began twirling in a move that became a solo dance to Flora, the angel statue relocated from Daisy's secret garden to the micro-island "second base" just behind Daisy. And his mind flashed on everything that had happened since that ridiculous miracle in the courtroom a year and a half ago.

First, Daisy has incorporated the Claude Squad as a public benefit Type "B" 501(c)(3) nonprofit corporation, with Monet's paintings and drawings as assets. Simon was the consensus President Emeritus of the Board of Directors, with Daisy as Keeper of the Treasure and Velocity as Secretary-General. Mel was the first Exalted Artist-In-Residence. Sam, at his request, assumed the title "Chief Security Sentinel-Avenger." With the Board in place, Daisy borrowed against the equity in the paintings (a hundred million plus) and the real work began.

HolParksDevCorp happily unloaded the Love Shack on the Claude Squad for what it had cost them plus ten percent, and Bronx Council Member Melissa Colfax helped Daisy purchase "Bojangles Field" from the New York City Housing Authority for twelve thousand dollars. Mel and Daisy were put in charge of rehabilitating the Love Shack, and Demo happily seized the daunting task of turning the tumbledown Negro League ballpark into Claude Monet's Dream Field.

Three months from the day they took title, the Moist Robots opened "Visions of Yankee Stadium by Claude Monet" at the refurbished Love Shack. This was an exclusive, timed-ticket art exhibit hosted by Melvin Flack, Artist. For a solid year, an average of 6,175 people a day paid eighteen dollars to chat up Mel and then bask in the crazy glory of Monet's paintings and drawings. Then a surprise: they stepped into a "Preview Center" called "Welcome to the Dream Field." This was Demo's immersive, multi-media sound and light show where Monet's Yankee Stadium materialized all around them and came to life. Before they left, these guests were invited to commemorate their visit with tote bag from the gift shop, a work from the Moist Robots Signature Gallery, and a Macadamia-Milk Double Latte from Claude's Coffee Corner.

Claude Monet's Dream Field opened to the public at noon on April 18th, the anniversary of the opening of (what should have been Claude Monet's) Yankee Stadium in 1923. The Moist Robot Art Collective had tripled in size to build the place, as Demo recruited hundreds of artists, painters, engineers, 3-D modelers, and landscape designers from local art and design schools. Monet didn't get his turntable, but the Claude Squad achieved just about everything else their benefactor dreamed of: the kaleidoscopic "cathedral" façade, the outfield haystacks backed up by the water lily fence (with the warning track reflecting pond), and the infield koi pond spanned by the bridge from first base to third. Daisy had her pitching mound and grandstand gardens to go with her rooftop garden atop the Love Shack. The "Monet's Table" Brasserie offered guests a vegan slant on French country cuisine (tofu quiche, chickpea ratatouille, etc.) supervised by MR Chef Bartholomew "Bean Sprout" Metcalfe. And Demo made certain the whole place was the ultimate clean-green LEED Platinum off-the-grid masterpiece of freeganistical sustainability, down to mini-windmills ringing the entrance and the composting toilets.

At 1 p.m. on that opening day, Melvin Durward Flack and Daisy Hudnutt-Parkes were joined in holy matrimony by the Right Reverend Kevin "Demolition" Stevens of the Universal Life Church. Mel dressed as Monet and Daisy dressed as Euphonia in her white dress with the emerald trim, veiled bonnet, and parasol. Guests were then ushered into the Simon Brittle Right Field Art Concourse, where Mel's wind-swept portrait of Daisy was unveiled. This concourse would henceforth be dedicated to works generated by inspired artists who made the pilgrimage to this place of artistic inspiration. The Claude Monet Left Field Concourse was the new home of Monet's original Yankee Stadium paintings and drawings. (The Love Shack reverted to being a freegan art collective albeit one that owned its own building. And Daisy had refurbished the "Eagle's Nest" as a love nest for her and Mel.). The party that first night went on till midnight, with Mel singing "Our Love is Here to Stay" and Simon winning an ovation for his flamboyant tango with Daisy.

And now here he was three months later, alone and happy amidst a few thousand aspiring painters, amateur gardeners, and art buffs on this balmy July night. Oh, and also lovers. This place had become the hipster hook-up capital of Gotham City, crushing the Observation Deck of the Empire State Building. Most popular selfie spot? The top of the Japanese Bridge at sunset, with the haystacks and water lilies in the background.

And Demo had become famous for blowing the whole thing up every weekend night at 8:45 p.m., fifteen minutes before closing.

Mel had spent his life making everything complex and impossible and it was all just a self-defeating mind storm of lies. *Love was something outside my reach. Art was something other people were good at. Happiness was a rumor, a foreign country I'd never visit.* All lies. Now he knew the secret. *The secret is there is no secret,* he thought. *There is nothing to get, nothing to chase, no mystery to solve, no one to envy, nowhere better than right here and nothing to do but what's in front of me. I can take as long as I want to make every picture as beautiful as I can.*

Try and fail. Walk, fall down, get up, walk better. Be good at not quitting.

All Claude Monet did – and all Mel did now – was *paint the light.* Simple, and so damn hard. Daisy had sewn a special pocket in his favorite pants so he could carry Monet's journal with him everywhere, just so he could consult his mentor any time he wished. *"See! Sketch! Paint! It never ends. It never turns out right. It never gets easier, only and always more difficult. The riddle of senseless ambition can never be solved. Fortunately, the furious productive contemplation of that riddle at dawn in my garden translating light into art is metamorphic, revealing a vision of the divine: not the capturing, just the vision itself. That must suffice."* Mel smiled. *And it does, always and forever.*

"Ready?" said Daisy. She'd changed out of her gardening clothes into her shimmery red-velvet tango-friendly evening frock. Mel could see the grounds crew pushing together the temp tango floor in centerfield as the four-piece all-female tango "orchestra" (accordion, guitar, bass, violin) arranged themselves.

"Ready."

Daisy waived at Demo, standing at a metal box on a light pole behind home plate. He pulled a lever, and fifteen hundred Chinese lanterns blinked on, bathing the field in a cherry-red glow. Applause. Demo bowed and headed toward the dance floor along with hundreds of others.

Mel nodded at the band. They struck up the favored tango tune of Claude and Euphonia (and Helen and Louie, and of course Mel and

Daisy), "Tango Jalousie." Mel wrapped himself around his bride and that familiar thrill of everything about her caused him to laugh out loud as they moved as one, becoming the tango. *It's all a dance*, he thought. *A beautiful dance to the music of time. And I'm going to dance every moment I can.*

THE END

ABOUT THE AUTHOR

R. Lee Procter has loved Impressionist art since he saw a show of Claude Monet's haystacks in the 1980s. He currently works as a writer in the themed entertainment business, creating museum exhibit, stadium tours, and guest narratives for brand homes. He's also worked in advertising and the cable television business. He stumbled across the idea for this book in the Metropolitan Museum of Art Book Store, when he saw Monet paintings selling next to antique baseball cards. Wait a minute... Yankee Stadium opened in 1923, Monet didn't die until 1926. He really could have designed it! If he did, what happened to his designs? This book answers that question. And celebrates Monet as an artist like no other.

NOTE FROM THE AUTHOR

Word-of-mouth is crucial for any author to succeed. If you enjoyed *Claude Monet Designs Yankee Stadium - A Love Story*, please leave a review online—anywhere you are able. Even if it's just a sentence or two. It would make all the difference and would be very much appreciated.

Thanks!
R. Lee Procter

We hope you enjoyed reading this title from:

BLACK ROSE
writing™

www.blackrosewriting.com

Subscribe to our mailing list – *The Rosevine* – and receive **FREE** books, daily deals, and stay current with news about upcoming releases and our hottest authors.
Scan the QR code below to sign up.

Already a subscriber? Please accept a sincere thank you for being a fan of Black Rose Writing authors.

View other Black Rose Writing titles at
www.blackrosewriting.com/books and use promo code
PRINT to receive a **20% discount** when purchasing.